# THE OTHER PART

## The Omens of Likhabali

# THE OTHER PART

## The Omens of Likhabali

Asokan K. P.

PARTRIDGE

**To order additional copies of this book, contact**
Partridge India
000 800 10062 62
orders.india@partridgepublishing.com

www.partridgepublishing.com/india

The other part.

| | |
|---|---|
| //Saraswati namasthubhyam/ varade kaamaroopinee/ vidyarambham karishyami/ sidhirbhavathu me sada/ | /Ekadantam mahakayam thaptha kanchana sannibham/ lambodaram vishalaksham vandeham gananayakam/// |

To

Amma          (My Mother who left us in childhood)
Kunjamma      (Mother who brought up so far)
Amma          (Mother-in-law who poured immense love)

And all Mothers.....

# ABOUT THE AUTHOR

**H**e was born in 1966 to a agriculture labor of a backward village of Kerala, a state of South India, he failed to pass out his 12<sup>th</sup> class, left his home to find a job towards the far away state of Arunachal Pradesh, a lovely state of North east India lying in the beautiful lap of Himalayas.

He left Arunachal Pradesh where he was working as Saw Mill Manager in 1999 and worked in Kerala, Maharashtra, Assam and Gujarat engaging himself in the capacity of Van sales executive, sanitary showroom manager, auto electric workshop holder, and now working again as Saw Mill Manager.

He loved plants and trees but was forced to find his source of income working in saw mills butchering trees...

He is married to Letha a tutor and has two sons Ashish Ashok and Adersh Ashok.

# ACKNOWLEDGEMENTS

**W**ay back in 1987, I left Kerala, my homely state which situated at the south west corner of India, with my friend, towards Arunachal Pradesh, known as the 'land of rising sun', situated at the north east tip of the country. I went along with my friend to Daporijo, the district head quarter of Upper Siang district which happens to be the bordering territory with China. I stayed there for about five months and was invited by a tribal entrepreneur who was also a political leader of that state to join his firm as employee in his office. Seeing a better prospect suiting to my minimal educational qualifications, I left Daporijo to join the new job at Likabali, a lovely place situated at the foothills of the district of West Siang.

I remained there till 1999.

Green, green and only lush green everywhere, stretches of hills with thick woods, deep valleys where white, foggy clouds resting in peace, and the hilly roads making sight of crawling snakes... at distant intervals, the tribal villages comprising adjacent dwelling houses suspended on timbers posts, walled by bamboos and thatched by tokku leaves...

Yes, Arunachal is a marvelous feast for your eyes through which your mind will be filled with natural freshness...

And the lovely Likabali, its innocent and caring people. I lived there almost more than a decade, enjoying every moment of it with colleagues and friends.

When I begun this work, the name Likabali was the first and only choice to name my imaginary village in mind. There also exist the two villages in reality, the Lika and Bali villages when you cross over the magnificent Gai River. I sincerely tender my thankfulness to the lovely people of Lika, Bali, Garu and Likabali and the whole of Arunachal Pradesh to let me have the beautiful names.

I could not leave without thanking sincerely Mr. Kardu Taipodia and family with whom I was engaged as an employee. My heartfelt thanks for them.

Meanwhile I would like to state authentically that the characters of this work of fiction have nothing to do with the people of Arunachal as the living style and customs of those Himalayan tribal people are absolutely different and unique in their traditions and followings. The characters created in this work are absolutely fictional and imagined and have nothing to do with anybody in this world.

Now it is my duty to turn towards the Western Indian state of Gujarat where I am now staying and working at a village called Mithirohar at Gandhidham, within the district of Kutch, bordering Pakistan.

I have immense pleasure to thank my boss Mr. Shashi Aggarwal and family especially Mr. Amit Aggarwal who is my immediate boss at Gandhidham for having me the privilege to serve them and to have got inspired to write this book during the intervals of my duties.

It will be a severe crime of omission and ingratitude if I not mention Mr. Manish Kumar Shukla, Mr. Radheshyam Mishra, Mr. Deepak Singh who were kind enough to guide me to deal with MS Word during the preparation of my work in that format. I sincerely thank them all for their support and helping hands.

And my regards and heartfelt thankfulness to M/S. Partridge India Ltd, Author Solutions, M/S. Thinkstock images...to make my lifelong dream into reality. The patience, promptness and kindness in hearing me and to respond with helpful directions in each and every steps of this effort....

I thank Mr. Jake Rivers, Mr. Racel Cruz, Ms.Emily Laurel, Ms. Gemma Ramos and every one at M/S. Partridge India Ltd. who were in contact with me and assisted throughout this effort and for filling within me the courage to go ahead with this work.

I am glad to thank Microsoft to enable me to avoid numerous quantities of papers which might have put forth in and ultimately thrown away to dust bins...if I did not chose the MS Word format to write this work.

At the last of this, I thank My beloved better half Letha, Ashish and Adersh my sons and all those who encouraged me so far.

Thanks to all once again.

Asokan.K.P.

# PART 1

# CHAPTER

**G**ood or bad, the omens were often there. Clear intimations in advance from God, as they believe, needs mind of truthful wisdom to decipher them. Mostly not deciphered by the ignorance of the preachers and rarely it were well read and obeyed by as to whom it were supposed to adhere. The untimely calling of a craw or a cock, presence of an owl in the evening on a banyan tree, the abnormal barking of the dogs looking skywards- such were some of the omens of fateful or cheerful out comings in that inhabitation.

It was a vast territory, named Likhabali; consists of numerous houses and widely spread fields. The Dhirs were in the domain of the village. They were the self acclaimed rulers. The rest of the inhabitants were to follow their suits. There were others like the traders and farmers who were so close and familiar with the Dhirs. The traders offered commodities and the farmers grains to the Dhirs on demand. So they were treated fairly by the Dhirs and were inducted in the village council to have their say in things which demanded resolutions.

A large pond filled with cold water was there to feed the crops and livelihood. But a major portion of the inhabitants of the village were barred from using the pond. They were the Adhirs, forced to dwell in the mere settlements made on the outskirts of the village. The settlements of Adhirs were made on the other side of the village road which made the boundary between the elite Dhirs and the peasant Adhirs. Men and women with children of the Adhirs forced to work whole day for the elites in their farms and fields and houses.

They were ordered to address the elite class with the words "MYLORD", "MYSAVIOUR" which were meant to address to gods or deities. Even the children should be addressed so, otherwise they will be punished for disrespect.

Banned to worship or pray, driven out from social ceremonies and compelled to live in ignorance and dirt. Not allowed to bath or wash in the pond and lived with the dirty water fetched from waste streams for food and wash.

So there existed another pond, invisibly filling over with the tears of sorrow originated from discrimination, oppression and injustice, searching to break the bunds around it at any available outburst.

On a shiny day evening in the spring, a strange guest reached there. Wearing a white turban on head, a long coat covering all his body down to feet; grey and long beards and a pair of sparkling eyes, the man looked attractive and special but strange to everybody who saw him. A bundle made as a bag out of cloth in his shoulder. The tall, old but strong man sat on the foundation made around the large banyan tree grown by the side of the middle path of Likhabali.

People began to gather around him. The village head along with his brother also present there. He enquired:

"Babaji, kindly let us know who you are"

"I am a mere creation of the almighty" said the old man showing his spread hands up skywards.

Irritated but in constraint, asked the head of the village: "where do you belong to?"

"I belong to where ever the Great God's name is praised"

"Why are you here?"

"To heel your ills"

Manab, the village head become silent for while. His brother, Heera got furious on the old man's words. But he has to show patience before his brother who is the head. He looked into his eyes. Seeing his brother remain confused, he called a fellow villager who stayed in the last row of the gathering. A pale mid aged man in skeletons came forward hesitantly and bowed. He was coughing in regular intervals.

"Heel him at once! He is ill" commanded Heera, the brother of Manab.

The old man smiled and said "bring some water."

Water, in a tumbler was served to him. He picked the tumbler with both hands and rose up to his face. With closed eyes, he chanted some rituals and said to the man he meant to heal;

"Take this along to your home and drink yourself and your family members from this before you sleep and come tomorrow"

The man came in front of him and received it after bowing with clabbed* hands and touching his feet.

"Do not bow to me. Bow only to the one and only Lord above."

There was a huge roar of murmuring amongst the gathered villagers. Manab, the head was wondering how courageous is this old man, lonely coming to a strange village and behave like a conqueror. He thought he needs to understand him before taking any actions. He said;

"Keep quiet," he ordered to the crowd and said "Babaji, please refresh yourself at the village rest house. We will meet tomorrow" and he directed the keeper of the rest house to treat him well according to the customs.

Then the gathering slowly began to disperse. And the day was creeping into the dark blankets of night.

---

* This is a word I propose to English language for the action of folding both palms of a human in respect of God or guests when they prays or welcome someone, a traditional practice among the Hindus in India.

# CHAPTER

T he tender morning rays of the sun were struggling to come through the veil of clouds spread in the sky over Likhabali. Contrary to yesterday, it might be a showery day in the offing. Thus were the faces of the gloomy clouds which seemed struggling to hold back tears. Nature itself resembled that something amiss is going to happen there.

Manab, the headman summoned a meeting of the village council in the morning. He wanted to make a consensus among the council members before dealing with the old man. The council consisted of seven members; the chief priest, being the president, Manab, Heera and the rest four from the folk of land lords and merchants of the village.

The meeting commenced with the prayer to the deity of the village by the priest. Then he demanded Manab to explain the reasons the meeting necessitated. The head of village rose and began to brief thus:

"One old man, alien to this village came here yesterday. On our queries, he replied arrogantly and claimed that he could heel all of our ills. Samba, one of the Adhir, the long ailing fellow of our village was presented to him to cure his diseases. He has been given a tumbler of water chanted by rituals by the old man and asked him to return today after consuming water at night.

The notable thing was that he is firm believer in God whatever might be his way of faith. His words were coming out straightly from his heart which is so powerful and convincing"

The chief priest said: "There were omens I felt that we are going to face abnormal things. Hard time is ahead and we must be restraint in our deeds. The almighty has many ways to nurture its creations and the world is so diverse that while practicing faith, man is compelled to accept various systems and ways to satisfy their own minds. So let's see what the man intends to do."

Heera said: "This is ridiculous. He must be punished and straightly driven out." The landlords were eager to support him but remained silent.

Manab said: "No my brother, don't be so short tempered. Obey our holy priest's words."

All the rest of the sitting council supported him, suppressing the thoughts of dissent. And thus they resolved to observe the old man's further behavior and actions.

As they approached the rest house, a huge crowd was already formed there. Children, women, old and young men comprised the crowd. All were in excitement and delighted and some were appealing aloud for his, the old man's grace and help to recover their various ailments. Humans are after miracles. Anything which happens against contemporary belief, custom and tradition became miracles to humans. The awaked may seek to link such miracles with logic and reality before coming to any conclusions but the major part, being and ignorant will fell into the charisma and wonders of extraordinary happenings.

Samba, an Adhir, the man who was served with water yesterday was seen in the feet of the old man along with his entire family. His face shining in delight, joyous smile in his lips and tears of joy in his eyes cried loud:

"This sacred soul has cured my decease! I was cursed to suffer for my entire life. Now I am fully recovered. My life is indebted to him!!"

The crowd cheered to his declaration and applauded the old man. They were mostly the men belonged to Adhir class.

Adhirs, comprising about one third of the total population had been a neglected part of that village. Deprived of better living and subjected to exploitation and compelled to work hard even day and night in the field, farms and households of the elite class.

For generations, they became almost deaf and dumb like animals having lost any sense of resistance or response. Sufferings, struggles, hunger and suppressions made them so ignorant and insensitive. Bonded lives they were, forgot even to aspire for relief.

The village head Manab as he was smooth in behavior and kind enough to help them when they needed it. His was a nature quite different from his ancestors. His words and deeds were mild. He did not consider them to be isolated from the mainstream. But the customs and precedence were so strong that his desire to make a change in them made so difficult. The Chief priest also knew of his mindset and he too was disturbed that injustice is being inflicted, purely against the true spirits of the principles of the scriptures of their ancestral faith. They even hinted often about it but also feared that any attempt to alter the customary traditions will bring revolt within the council and order of the village.

On the contrary, Heera, who was adamant that the tradition to be kept forward intact. A trained fighter he, entrusted to defend the village in any eventuality, provided with other fighters to his command, and always aggressive, his actions caused harm to many. Rough and cruel to the Adhirs, he exploited them severely. Tortured their men and children and molested their ladies and daughters at any available moment. Many children have paternity attributed to him within Adhirs. He also inspired his men in command to molest Adhir women and girls and happily they enjoyed to rape and assault them rampantly. Those who were his victims were living with their anger and hate concealed within them.

Everybody, including Meena, his fair wife, knows it well. She was a neglected wife. Living in despair, having four children, she hated him too much.

Lala, the merchant, having his business near the bungalow of Heera was young and handsome. He liked her very much. Her fair looks and lovely statures attracted him. He felt solidarity with her heart and often tried to communicate. Whenever he tried to do so, she tried to avoid him, against her minds willingness. A woman, married against her wishes though, is not at all supposed to love another man. She has to concede to her fate and live according to the age old customs and traditions.

But the lust for love and care begun to grow in her everyday and the hatred against Heera surged in every moments of her life. The love she shed on the children and their affections gave some relief to her sufferings. Lala's frequent request for love had compelled her to have an affair with him secretly which was growing every day.

# CHAPTER

**T**he pond began to damage the bunds itself. Such was the pressure of the flooded tears of disgust and oppressions that the entire bund built around the invisible pond shattered at once. A mere old man with no arms and shields just made that miracle. Not a drop of blood, no physical harms and no combats. Delightful cries and praises to the Baba were stopped when the furious words screamed from Heera:

"keep quite you devils and bastards!" The crowd stunned for a moment and looked towards Baba.

"What black magic have you performed upon him and the folks?" Heera asked again.

Baba rose from his seat on the veranda of the rest house and said with a smile of tease:

"go and send your brother and the priest. I don't want to converse with you, for you are not my counterpart."

This furthered his wrath and he took out his sword from its scabbard.

"No Heera! Put it back! We are here and will talk to him". Manab shouted. Dissented but in compulsion, he acceded to his brother.

Then Manab turned to Baba and asked:

"Old man, what are you doing here? This is our traditional area possessed from the time unmemorable. Nobody ever attempted to encroach here and tried to disturb the peaceful life prevailed here. What instigate you to provoke us? We have our own way of faith and living supported by our holy scriptures. Nowhere in the world there is a place where are ills or ailments exempted. You claim to heal all of our ills. Are you the almighty God himself? Are you so much overconfident to attain parity with God? It is better that you leave at once or you must face punishment for the guilt of encroachment and instigating the people against the authority."

Baba said:

"Oh ignorant man, I am doing what is bound upon me by humanism and wish of God that is already bounding you too. You don't possess anything, even the soil under your feet where you are standing but only insane mind. All belong to Him who created. You should edit your mindset on tradition based on your belief.

"Belief is just an ever accumulating bundle when it lends blind eyes to adapt with ever evolving advancements of time.

"Huge bundles filled with the dirt of crime of past are not tradition but are accumulating burdens. You cannot have peace put on the jaws of a volcano which is set to erupt. Look in to the face of these poor helpless fellows. Can you see any sign of peace on them? I don't bother what is in your scriptures. You are glorifying a few things to hide the numerous crimes committed on your brotherhood. I shall remain with them if they desire so. Nothing can prevent me except their negation. You better ask them."

The crowd shouted in unison:

"He will not go, he will stay with us."

Jubilant in the suddenly gifted courage of rays of freedom, emitted through the words of the old man, they felt salvaged and looked so cheerful that they can face and crush anything, anybody comes against the irresistible flow of the newly found outbreak.

The wind started to blow there with a whistling from the tree tops. The dark clouds above began to pour its long held tears and an owl was sighted on the branch of the large banyan tree which was noted by the priest and he shouted:

"Clear out of the premises near the tree. It's danger coming!"

People heard him and began to clear out in panic. A thunder stroke and at once and the huge banyan tree split itself apart from top to the down stem in the middle and feel down to earth in two opposite directions. Stunned scared and in disbelief, everybody ran to seek shelters except the Baba and Head Priest, they stood in that stormy rain and exchanged their sights, both came closer:

"Welcome to you, the man sent by Destiny!"

Said the priest and continued: "forgive me if you can for the sins I committed in neglect the wishes of God. Good bye!"

And he went into the blindness of night. He was no more seen ever in the village again.

When Heera stepped in to his home, he found the children crying. When he asked, they said:

"Mother left us forever. She asked our forgiveness for doing so."

He cursed her and abused loudly. And called ten men under his command and said:

"Go, quick, to trace her and her companion and bring back alive or dead".

His anger was at its peak and he went straight to Manab and shouted:

"Your inability and coward deeds are the root cause of all this happenings. You don't deserve to be at the reigns of this village".

And as his hands went to pick up the sword, a serpent emerged there.

Serpents, worshiped as God in Likhabali, were considered as the rebirth of the ancestors of the inhabitants especially that of the village head. Nobody ever tries to beat or kill a snake when spotted but pray to them in fear and reverence. But the approaches of Adhirs were in contrary to it. They used to kill snakes in hide.

Stepped back in fear sat on his knees and clabbed his hand and he prayed:

"Forgive, forgive me My lord! Pardon me for my misconduct. I will not repeat thus."

Manab too prayed in his knees:

"Pardon him your Holiness, pardon him."

Then the serpent crawled outwards and Manab said:

"Heera, my brother, look into your own past actions and consult your conscience with honesty to get your answers. I am no more interested to continue here, but I have to do something before I quit. You just wait up to next evening."

Head held down, Heera withdrew with more revengeful wrath. He became a man with wounds inflicted on his pride and passions from the dual attacks suffered in head and heart by the Adhirs and Meena.

Manab exited from his home and went straight to the priest's seat. He cannot find him there but a scripture on a dry palm leaf, which said:

**"Bifurcate the village, give them their dues. Don't waste your time in search of me."**

In Disgust, Manab came back home. He felt tiresome, solitude and frustration. Mind filled with sorrow and guilt, he went to bed. The only consolation to him was the loving care and kind words of Janu, his wife. She had already brought home the four children from Heera's home and consoled them in their grief and assured to look after them like her own Children. Devoted to the heritage, she wondered how a mother like Meena can abandon her children for her selfish good pastures. She was aware of the neglect and violence meted out to Meena by Heera.

Before being slept, Manab decided to make up his mind to calms itself as he has to declare something which was painful and tough.

# CHAPTER

The other day broke in Likhabali with normal glare. But the minds of its inhabitants were anxious. Those who resided in the left part were the Adhirs and right side of the village occupied by the near and distant or far-distant relatives of the village head, landlords and merchants. It was a clear pre-classified division to avoid mingling with the other class. There was agriculture fields spread around except in the west, where barren lands and way to the nearest village lied. There were barren lands, after the agricultural fields.

The pond was situated almost in the middle, near the dividing road but right to it. Like its inhabitants, including humans, animals and all other living beings, it seemed that the entire inhabitation were keen to observe what is destined to them further. Elders, youngsters, children from both genders were more curious.

In the absence of the priest, it was impossible to hold the council as such was the precedence. Manab conveyed to all the other members to be present at the field along with the elders and important members of the village at around ten o'clock in the morning. He knew that the declaration he intends to make before the meeting will surely against the like and taste of his own men but the other part will applaud. He decided to face whatever be the outcome.

Manab rose to speak when the gathering swelled in the field where the split banyan tree was still lying like the torn apart body parts of a huge giant. People were kept themselves far away from it fearfully.

"My dear village men, for the past several decades constituting many centuries, we were living in this beautiful village, Likhabali. Gifted with vast area of fertile fields of agriculture and dwellings, we were making our livelihood according to the customs and traditions we were inherited from the ancestors believing that traditions were in the true spirit of the scriptures bestowed upon to us by the ancient forefathers. However, I am not sure that such customs and traditions were according to the scriptures as I am not a scholar having full knowledge of them but we were dependent on the Priests who were intended to have studied them and supposed to have advised us according to their true spirit and intensions.

'Honestly speaking, I doubt the followings so far were truthful and sincere to the scriptures as my own conscience disapproved the same for many times during my short span of tenure in the village as its headman. Unfortunately the priest who was in the seat was also seemed with my own tunes of thoughts and I think he was feeling guilty about it and sought to impose his self in exile. The sinful actions of our past and present towards our own brethren have forced us today to suffer in the unity and integrity of Likhabali.

'Today, I feel that it is time to answer to the unheard questions, the brutalities committed and to the injustice imparted. I know well that everybody amongst us will not confirm or consent this facts and surely they revolt. But I am determined in my actions and decisions, giving due heed to my heart.

'Destiny has brought here a sage. Sages never are selfish or ill wished. I sincerely apologize to him for the past and warmly welcome him to the future course of this village. His clear and truthful wisdom will lead them who follow him. And hereunto, in all your witness, I declare thus:

**"The village of Likhabali is hereby bifurcated. The left side of it will here in after known as Bali village and the rest as Likha village. Both will have separate domains and fates according to their own separate whips of reigns of their choices."**

Uproars, protests, screaming's, applauds and disbelief.....mixed reactions rose from the crowd.

"What foolishness is this?"

Heera said to the land lords standing near to him with utmost hate and anger towards his brother, crushing his teeth.

He was also looking for the men whom he sent in search of Meena and Lala. There was no any news of tracing them yet. It doubled his fury and wished to destruct all his opponents.

"Thank you,"

Said Baba "for your magnanimous declaration for giving the deprived their rightful dues. I, on their behalf, assure you that they will not be in enmity towards your men. But in case of aggressions meted out to them, they surely will retaliate and the consequences will be distasteful to the aggressors. Please advice your men to behave gently. I know that you have enough men trained in arms and combat. Do not underestimate these poor Adhirs who lacks such skills that they could be easily conquered."

It was decided to make necessary set ups and arrangements for the demarcation of boundaries and possession of lands and agricultural fields.

Manab announced further:

"Since the village is not in existence, the post of mine as its Head also turns extinguished. Now Likha and Bali will have their own heads according to their choices. Thanking you all for suffering me so far."

With folded hands he retired and went straight to the vacant seat of priest, where he prayed until late night.

# CHAPTER

The new dawn broke into Bali with delightful shine. Weather was pleasant and the dwellers jubilant. Adhirs, availing unexpected sudden freedom were confused a lot on many things. They were ignorant of almost everything except hard work and eating and mating with their life partners.

Baba knew all this. He called them every day to advice them and directed them to teach what they learned from him all other members of the society. He began to gather men, women, youth and children and divided them into groups comprising twenty five members and made one each to its leader. The leaders will learn from him and they will impart what they learn from Baba to his group members. He taught about healthy living, eating, reading, farming and how to grown up children.

He also taught physical training to them for self-defense. Two groups of youngsters created with Mitu leading the male and Gori as the female part. They will create a force consisting all the youths of Bali. Mitu was the son of samba who was Baba's first disciple and Gori, daughter of Kaliya and Matu.

Matu was a victim of Heera. She brutally raped by him several a times due to her fair looks. Gori was the outcome of such a rape. Her paternity goes to Heera. She was aware of this and was very much disturbed when some fellow of the folk remarks about it or somebody teases on the subject. Her mind filled with anger and sometimes vowed to take revenge on that rascal who caused her cursed birth. She was in her post teen ages and her looks were quiet nice and attractive. With sparkling eyes and the face reflecting determination, she was almost exceptional out the other girls in that folk.

She was very keen on the lessons and trainings got from Baba. Never missed any sessions and devoted her entirely in severe practices and teachings. She easily and speedily excelled in archery. Arrows from her bows were sharp in hitting the targets. She also learned in swords with amazing skills which stunned everybody including Baba. Baba was just orally training her due to his old age but she picked every of his words in its soul and spirits.

She also proved a very good teacher in imparting what she learned. Very strict in discipline, she never tolerated any kind of fouls from her fellows and punished severely on every lapses. She speaks loudly and clearly with words and its intentions spearing in to every ear in depth. Having no soft sentiments, her speeches inspire them a lot to follow her orders.

Mitu the youngster was in a habit of glaring at Gori at every available moment and lost in thought without paying any attention to the sessions. Gori noted it and asked him to concentrate his trainings. He smiled and shook his heads in consent but continued the habit. Gori minded never.

One evening after the sessions, she approached Baba and asked: "Baba where are you coming from?"

"Daughter, I am coming from the hills in the north"

"From the hills, where are hills and what were you doing there?"

"It is in the northern direction, filled with forest almost covered in white snow. With animals and birds of many kinds"

"What were you doing there?"

"I was meditating and praying in search of truth and god"

"Where did you stay there?"

"There are caves in the hills. I chose one to dwell my body"

"Have you got them?"

"Honestly if I say, I did not get all my answers which I sought. My mind instructed me to live the rest of my life with humans where a lot could I can understand"

"Are you a magician?"

"Why are you asking this?"

"Because you performed magic and healed Samba"

"No child, it is not magic. I just gave him medicated water."

"But we don't see any medicine you put in the tumbler"

"Yes, you or the other may have not seen it. But when I asked for the tumbler, everybody diverted their eyes from me. Then I picked a pinch of herbal powder from my pocket of my coat I wore and kept it in between my fingers and dropped in the water when the tumbler handed over to me. Look, no wonder can treat an ailment over a night. You have to have faith in the doctor when you are being treated and should be always positive. Further you must maintain healthy habits in life to keep your body away from diseases."

"And what was about the fate of banyan tree?"

"It was not a miracle. Its inside was rotten and thus weak. The huge weight of its branches and leaves caused the tree's split and it's was in its old ages. The wind, blown then caused fall it down. You can look it right now that the split stems are rotten inside which is still lying there."

"The omens and their meanings; are they truthful?" She asked.

"Daughter, I am not sure about it. Do not expect anybody who can answer every question. Perceptions and experiences of humans tested with their understandings create ones view on such things. Try to make your own perceptions after intercepting the things with your knowledge and wisdom. Chose your faith with the approval of your mind and heart not by compulsion or allured.

She relieved her mind and asked further:

"Do you know about any other thing which could be used in conflicts?"

She asked with great zeal.

Smiled the Baba and said:

"Of course, there is a thing I know called gun powder. It is used by progressed men who uses during wars and invasions"

"Can we get it from somewhere?"

"Here, it is impossible. But we must ask the merchant who runs the shop in our village whether he can provide it to us. I will enquire and arrange for it if it is available to him"

She was impressed with his assurance. And with a deep thought she walked to her home. When she was returning, Mitu was staying in the middle of her way.

"What happened, Mitu?" She asked.

"I want to talk to you" he said and gleamed for awhile.

"Say it out, I want to go."

"Gori", he called in mild and said hesitatingly with a reddish face "I love you." And he looked into her face with expectation.

She glared him thoroughly and replied straight:

"What stupidity are you saying? I am not after any of such silly sentiments. Do not try ever to speak me like these unwanted and waste full things. Keep it in your mind and if you are so much in need of such passions, try other girls. Our village is not out of girls." And she rushed to her home in haste and hate.

Ashamed, as he got a sudden slap on face, Mitu stood there, in despair and he exclaimed:

"What is her heart built up with? Is it is out of rocks or wood?!" Then he went towards his hut.

# CHAPTER

**L**ikhabali was situated in a remote, isolated area from other villages. It maintained borders with a vast lake in its three sides and the rest one and only border connecting it with Maji village at some distant far. The road to the rest of the world went through Maji followed by Garu. They have more connections with the Garu in trades and trainings for its people as Garu was advanced in their lifestyles and awareness. Garu got nearness and sudden access to the mainland state.

Maji maintained hostility towards Likhabali and kept its eyes on it in greed and envy for its fertile agricultural lands and vegetation. It has the privilege of having large pools of water with the surrounding lakes to feed the crops.

The separation process went on without too much hurdles except about the pond. Since it situated within right side comprising Likha village, they did not consent to depart it to the other side or to share the water. But water was needed everywhere, to drink, bath and to feed cattle and farms. Finally, Baba proposed that Bali will dig one pond for itself and his men were persuaded and vowed to make one urgently. They began to dig the field just opposite to the existing one.

Samba was made the head of village. He was the first disciple of Baba and was very much learned than the other fellows due to his proximity with Baba. Adhirs made a hut with bamboos and straws for Baba with swiftness and he began to reside in it and healed the patients with his herbals and continued to teach and train them.

The debris of the banyan tree was cleared by the Adhirs. Two siblings were budded out of its roots and began to grow together. Nobody disturbed its growth. The mother roots provided them with the cereals needed.

Nothing is lost for ever and nothing decays in vain.

In Likha, Heera made as the headman. There were no any contenders for the post. Even if anybody dared to content, Heera was determined to thwart any such moves. He has to revenge a lot to calm his disturbed mind.

"Don't underestimate these poor Adhirs..." those words of that old man still resonate in his ears...

Manab spent most of his daytime in the priest's room where the old scriptures were kept. He began to devote his head and heart in studying them one by one. There were large bundles of them made up of dried palm leaves. At the outset, he felt difficulty in understanding them but he do not quit. Read and read them several times until he was clear on the subjects it contented. He prayed and meditated in leisure times and went to home only at nights.

Heera on the other hand, was eager to settle his scores with the Adhirs and wished to eliminate them from the face of earth. His frustration furthered when the men whom he sent in search his wife were returned empty hand. He reprimanded them severely for the failure.

Heera underwent in long deliberations with his faithful aids comprising some landlords and merchants about the future plan of actions. Being a trained fellow he did not underestimate his enemies though their experiences in conflicts were very poor.

"Friends, we have to make a detailed plan to counter them": Heera said.

"Yes Heera, now our morals are in its lowest and the leading fighters are tired enough in their unsuccessful journey who returned in despair." said Lakha the landlord.

"Let them rest for some days. We have to gather more arms and further training is necessary to boost up their morale."

"Then get them arranged; the arms and trainers" – Lakha said.

"You know, some of the Adhirs are still staying with us who were loyal to brother Manab. We have to utilize them in our plans without hinting it to them. We must restrain ourselves while dealing with them that no harm may cause to them. Be lavish on them in terms of money or food."

"Yes yes, we should attract some more of them from the other side to destabilize them" said Maza, the merchant and continued:

"There will be very shortage for labor men to work in our farms and houses. Otherwise we would be compelled to bring in labors from the far distant villages"

"You are right. Our farms and cattle and household will suffer. It will not be wise to anticipate defection from the Adhirs but have to arrange alternatives to meet the challenge"

"Yes, I am going to sent for the nearest village to bring some working men and women"

"We should always be watchful on their activities. Some should be deployed to spy on them"

"Right, I will look into it. And you all help me to provide reliable men for that"

"All right" said all and the meeting disbursed.

Soon after reporting to Heera some of his men went to the Bali village for their lady hunt. The elders of almost all the houses were busy at digging the pond. So, most houses were left with children and girls who were engaged in preparing meals for the workers. Finding the opportunity the lady hunters raped the girls with wild enthusiasm and left the village before any elders comes back from their works. When the elders came, they knew the incident and were got angry and reported to the Baba and Head, Samba. Baba summoned his leaders of all groups and said:

"Look, this is a matter of grave concern and it is sensitive too. I suggest you to tackle this issue by yourselves."

"But how is it possible Baba? You have already said that there will be no aggressions from our side.

"And our trainings are not yet completed": said Mitu.

"You must remember that I did say to the Dhirs that they will be retaliated in the event of their invasions. Trainings will never complete till your lifetime. So will you suffer all their atrocities till the completion of you trainings?" asked Baba.

"But we need your help to devise any strategy"

"No. How long will you depend on others on every issues coming in your way? You have to think about them yourselves. Once you win in your strategy you will be inspired by that victory and will be more confident forever. So go and think collectively and make some plans. Please keep in mind that you are going to strategize against men who are well trained and have more strength in arms and combat. Employ your brains than your sentiments while making any plan of actions."

"Alright, thank you Baba, we are going to do it."

Said Gori in confident tones and called the rest to her home.

Baba smiled. He fore sawn that this young girl is a gift to this village as she holds enough materials within her to do wonders. He recognized it in the first sight of her.

'She will supersede everybody and will bring glory to their folk' He thought. And he was glad that he had arranged to get the gun powder from the merchant. He will bring it in his next trip to the market in the nearby village within two or three days.

The merchant Manik was allowed settle within Bali as soon as the division occurred. He was eagerly looking for it. He belonged to the Maji village with which the Dhirs have enmity day back to about three decades. The then village head of Maji was lured by the fertile vast lands of Likhabali. He tried in vain once to capture the village as the brave fighters of Likhabali lead by Heera gave a bitter replay. Since then, no villager of Maji was ever allowed to settle in Likhabali with any ventures. Manik was a trader and close to the village head of Maji and he was keeping an eye on the on goings in Likhabali. During the courses of happenings after Baba's arrival, he even instigated the Adhirs to stand united behind Baba. He was granted permission to settle with his trade in return. So Manik was always ready to help the Adhirs at any cost as directed by his own village head.

# CHAPTER

**B**aba called Gori and said:

"Your gun powder will come within two days. Make your plans to utilize when you feel it is necessary"

"Baba, I want to learn about it in detail. I will come back to you when our meeting in my home will be over."

She sprinted with joy to home to conduct the meeting. Her heart was filled and thrilled with excitement for having got the gun powder. But not mentioned about it to anybody.

She selected some households from her village which will have potential threat of molestation from the Dhir fighters. She said the people gathered to bring the ladies from the selected homes. When all arrived, Gori stood and spoke:

"Enough we have suffered. My dear people, now the time has came to reap a bumper crop. The seeds were bowed, grown and become ripe enough, at the expense of our humanity. They have ploughed up the moral fields of our womanhood and bowed the seeds of their sinful arrogance and suppressions, nurtured with our tears and blood. Now grind your sickles to its utmost sharpness to reap the whole sinful crops of their exploitations and atrocities. If fails to reap it at this ripe time, we will lose for ever our rights to live in proud and dignity. Fill your hearts with strong determination. No Gods are there to help us in our miseries except their glare with blind eyes and hear with deafened ears as we used to experience so far. So prepare your minds and hands to do what I am suggesting to you now:

She stopped for a while and said:

"Please get out all of you except whom I mark to stay within."

And she spelled fifteen names of ladies who seemed courageous and good looking. All exited but remained the fifteen. Then she closed the doors and started to instruct them within the room. Motivated by her touching words, all were become enthusiastic and longed to do something to defend their identity and survival.

Once she explained them what they were intended to do, she asked them:

"If anyone amongst you are not ready or afraid to do what I said, should withdrew from the mission now itself. And anybody despite their assurance fails will be severely punished. So make it clear now before we leave. There is no compulsion from me to you to proceed with but once you agreed, you must adhere to the mission."

Nobody replied. All were prepared to do what she instructed. With a cheer of solidarity to everybody, she disbursed the sitting and came out and spoke to the awaiting people:

"So dears, our first mission has commenced from now onwards. I know that you all stayed outside are curious to what were went on inside. But in the sake of success of our mission it is necessary to keep it secret for a while. You all will know its details later on. Please be co-operative and patient and prepare for the best"

"Yes daughter, we all has full trust in you. Go ahead. Our hearts and minds are always with you" said the elders from the gathering.

Then she went to Baba. He elaborated about the character and nature of the gun powder to her in details.

How it is being in use to make explosives and in weapons. She was thrilled and impatient to get it experimented. But Baba cautioned her about its dangerous aspects also and warned to keep vigilance while deciding to use the powder.

# CHAPTER

## 8

The digging of pond was getting to be finished. They made a boundary wall along the border with Likha village with the clay mud excavated out from the digging site.

At Gori's insistence, there made another false fencing made up of dry woods inside the mud wall. The inside fake wall blocked straight entry through the gateway. Anybody who enters should have to turn right or leftwards through a narrow passage for about thirty feet to enter the village. Big bamboos having thick shells brought and filled with the gun powder along with small rock chips with sharpened edges and nails were inserted within the bamboos by drilling its knees and the holes were closed tightly leaving cords immersed in the powder outwards. That long bamboos were placed all along the length of the fencing in the middle and the fencing were packed with dry leafs and straws. Stone pillars installed in distances to strengthen the fencing for it might not fell in winds. This fencing virtually blocked the entrance through the main gate directly. Anybody enters or exits needed to walk sideways up to the extent of the false fencing's length. The villagers felt embarrassed on this extra strain in transit but kept quiet assuming its significance in their safety. Two watching towers were also made on both ends of that fencing in safe distances and two men entrusted to guard in it always.

Gori began another mission. She encouraged Adhirs to collect puppies and grow them in every household. She strictly said to name their dogs after "MYLORD" or with "MYSAVIOUR". The villagers began grow dogs and all of them named as she said. When a stranger spotted, dogs barked violently and by calling their name they will be calmed. Dogs were trained not to bark on the Adhirs. For which it was decided that every member of the village should mingle with every family routinely to make them familiar to the dogs. So the meeting venues of the groups were shifted alternatively to cover every household.

On the other part, at Likha, Heera went to a tour to the distant village, Garu to get some trainers for his men. Beera, the elder son of Manab was undergoing his training in arms and learning's at the same village which was in fame for its warrior skills. Beera is expected to complete his mission within a year. Heera met the head of the village and informed his purpose. The headman kept a warm relationship with the family of Manab. So he made Heera happy by providing what he sought. He also arranged scores of workmen for the farms.

Beera knew about his uncle's arrival. He met him and offered his respects and enquired about the happenings of his family and village. Heera detailed everything to him and asked him to not bother about and concentrate in his studies. Then he returned.

While returning home, Heera glared at the households of Adhirs in search of ladies. It went a long days he got his flesh hunt due to the unexpected incidents in the village and in his own life. His urge for sex grown within him unbearably. To his excitement, he saw the Adhir ladies in a strange and fair looks having jasmine flowers ornamented on their hairs and clad in attractive robes. Those sights lured his mind. His accompanying men also noted this. They decided to raid the village in the evening.

Gori got the news of the return of her opponents. She sent signals to every members of the group of the mission and strictly said to implement the directives. She deployed her fellows outside the mission group to watch every household she marked and said to report to Mitu whether the house was visited by Heera's men.

The day went to sleep in the darkness. Bali's determined ladies were waiting for their harvest. They were looked so attractive that any men would be lured to mate with them.

Amongst the fifteen members in mission, thirteen got their subjects. Heera chose to visit Shila's home. He was treated with the violent barking of the dog in front of the house. He stunned in fear and called out for help. He was suffering from fear out of the sight of dogs since his childhood. He hated that creature with terrible fear. The only fear he possessed in his valiant nature. There were no dogs grown in their households. Rarely some street dogs strayed often which were arrived from far villages in search of food or mates. Once it happened to encounter a big dog that barked aloud at him and he ran around with tremendous fear seeking somebody rescues. An elder man came by helped him to drive out the dog. That experience horribly hunting him till today. It was after a long time that he seen a barking dog now.

Shila said from his house loudly that she is changing her dress after bathing. And she said again loudly:

"My Lord, call the dog by its name and it will be quite."

"What's its name?" Angry Heera enquired.

"Call it by 'My Savior', that is its name, otherwise it will bite you badly."

Reluctant but in compulsion seeing the beauty of Shila, he yelled:

"My Savior, go out of my way you cursed!" The dog kept calm.

Then Shila came out with a smile in hide and called the dog to keep quite.

Everymen who visited the village in quest of women bodies were met with the same experience. They were welcomed warmly by the well looked ladies after the frightening experience with the dogs and directed to their beds inside. The homes were almost empty except the women as pre planned. The ladies embraced them and lead to their beds and themselves initiated to make them disrobe. They fore played for long time and made their genitals erected to their peaks. And the men were impatient to have intercourse. As soon as they got to full erections, the ladies suddenly took out the sharpened sickles from their bedsides and grabbing their erected penises, reaped the organs quickly and thrown out the flesh pieces from the windows!

With terrible pain and horror, the men, screamed and grabbed their robes available and placed them to hide the wounded, bleeding secret part of body and sprinted out of the homes. The dogs wildly barked, chased and driven them out of the houses. Their running tracks were marked by the lines made up of droplets of bloods spilled out through their hands clutching the robes...

Meanwhile, Shila had a terror within her when she saw him when the dog barked. She did not expect him as her visitor. She heard that he was excellent in his body actions in fighting's. As she welcomed him into her bed, she was trembling with fear and Heera pulled her towards him and began his games on her. Owing her husband's impotency and lack of interests, she was longing for sexual pleasures for a long period. She thus submitted herself to him wholly and enjoyed the mating. The thought of her duty entrusted to her never came into her mind during the intercourse. Thus Heera escaped the assault of the mission group.

In the very earliest hours of the day, Gori called her observers and enquired:

"How many were they?"

"Thirteen", said Mitu who gathered the reports.

"Anybody escaped the attack?"

"One of them, Heera, their Headman"

"Who was his host?"

"Shila"

Gori's eyes became red in fury. She summoned Shila and other mission members to Baba's hut urgently. She was trembling with anger. She cannot tolerate failure.

When the members of the mission gathered, she appreciated everyone who was victorious and appealed to keep their spirits motivated from the victory. And she turned to Shila and enquired:

"What happened to you the shameless traitor?"

"Forgive me daughter, I was feared a lot. It was the Head himself. I heard a lot about his fightings....."

"Did he come there for a fight?"

"I did not expect Heera. I was fully prepared to deal with any other fellows. I got nervous sighting him and was compelled to surrender before his enormous strength."

"I had already said you all that men of any strength are slaves in bed with a woman when they are aroused. You did not heed my words and went for your greed and bodily pleasures and put on stake the success of a noble mission. You were not bothered about the miseries of our past. You cheated all of us and our just begun journey towards a dignified and decent life. You are a traitor."

Shila began to cry. With folded hands she prayed for forgiveness.

"Not ever! You will be punished identically so that nobody in this new born village will ever attempt to cheat in the future."

And she appealed to the Baba and Samba to award severe punishment to Shila.

Baba said

"You suggest your action of punishment because you were the mission maker."

"Expel her from the village along with family with shaved heads. She has no moral right to stay here anymore."

All of them approved her words and ordered to shave off the heads of every member of Shila's family.

"Now, don't be jubilant in the victory over Heera's men. He became a wild beast now and will surely strike back. Anything dreadful could happen. So let's be prepared for it."

She asked them to pour the gun powder all along the false fencing. Strictly instructed the trained fighters to keep their arms ready and stuck to their assigned positions. Elders, women and children were said to keep themselves within their houses.

"Next two or three days will be crucial. Please keep in touch with your respective group leaders. I will send you the directions in time. Don't be panic. We are capable enough to take on them."

Heera returned his home with an unhurt body but his dignity and pride were hurt by the encounter with the dog. 'What a cunning scheme the bastards made to insult us!' he thought.

"I will kill whole of the bastards and bury them with their damned dogs."

He murmured and crushed his teeth in anguish. He heard about the tragic incident suffered by his men during their raids at Bali. His wrath and temper rose to its peaks. He arranged for their treatment. Everybody was moaning is extreme pain and somebody have faded down with continuous bleeding and fear of death. He tried to console them and vowed that he will do his best to save their lives. He summoned the best physicians available and provided with what herbs required to heal the assaulted.

In the meantime he asked the fighters within his command and the men who come from Garu to prepare an attack plan at the earliest. He was getting humiliated every moment as there were complaints from the women, children and elders who were compelled to address the dogs of Adhirs with phrases of high esteem and respects. They only used to hear them from the Adhir's for the time immemorial and used only to offer prayers their deities.

Manab was informed of every detail by his wife but made no response at all. He has become more withdrawn day to day…and the snakes lived in Likha were also silent and kept living on calmly. The two sibling of the banyan tree were also quietly growing like mute spectators but impassionate.

# CHAPTER

**9**

hila who was expelled from Bali along with her family sought asylum in Likha. Meanwhile, Heera, despite being irritated by the dog episode, received her and granted shelter and settlement in Likha. All of their heads shaved and insulted by their own men felt some relief in Likha as the behavior of the elite class has been mild and compassionate.

Two men out of the twelve were hurt, succumbed to death to their bleedings. The physicians could not escape them despite their every attempt.

Both sides were waiting. The Likha village was looking forward to unleash a terror of revengeful strike back at ripe time available and Bali to retaliate.

Alongside, the farming fields of both villages are looking towards their masters for their maneuvers on them to get prepared for the seasonal crops. Baba advised his men to get ready for the farming. They were, in their whole history of inhabitation in that place, have become the true owners of pieces of land. Yet they did not realize its significance.

The thrill and pride felt in possessing lands gives man immense pleasure. The Pieces of the part of earth which revolves around the mighty sun; which creates day and nights; pieces of soil in which humans along with trillions of other living creatures and nonliving objects born, thrive to survive with others in amity and enmity. They were deprived of feeling that experiences so far. So the experience of possession of a piece of land was strange to them.

And they began to start with plough. Cattles were rare in their possession. They had tendered the works in those fields till the past in compulsion. Now it is their need. Baba knew its significance and he motivated them.

"Bring your hearts in your hands while you work. It will gift you tremendous satisfaction":

Baba inspired them to do every work with sincere devotions. Since they lacked seeds, Baba arranged to bring from outside with the help of the merchant.

The farmers of Likha village started their farming earlier than Bali with their traditional splendor by the help of labors remained with them and with whom they brought from outside. They have had enough facilities in their command and custody. And they do have the experience of farming traditionally. So they were the first to bow the seeds.

Heera planned a plot. The old pond was filled with fish. He engaged some of the labors brought from Garu to catch fishes. And he said them:

"Take it along to Bali village. Nobody in Likha eats fishes. You may sell it in Bali and keep the money with yourselves. But just say if anybody questions that you catch the fishes in hide."

With the huge catch of fish from the pond, they went to sell fishes in Bali. They were welcomed there by the horrible bark of the dogs. Having been familiar with dogs they thrown out tiny fishes from their catch to the dogs. Villagers surrounded the fish sellers and delighted to see their favorite dish and bought the fishes and asked them to come whenever they got fishes. Fish sellers agreed and assured to come again with catches. Heera was eager to enquire about the response on their return. They reported what he required and said them:

"You will catch fishes regularly and sell it in Bali. You will have all the money earned from the selling."

They thanked him with hearts filled in happiness and went to their camps with minds dreamt of swelling wallets.

Some days passed. The fish sellers were happily sold and earned money. One day a man out the fish sellers was summoned by Heera in his home when he was passing his leisure time at the camp. Heera took out a bundle filled with money and handed over to him. The greedy man was excited and enquired:

"My lord, what is for this you doing this magnanimity to me?"

Heera then whispered him something in detail. After hearing all that he said in astonishment:

"Your majesty, I am afraid, I cannot do it"

"You must!" Heera said and continued "You will have all this if you do what I asked or will be finished" and he rubbed in the handle of his sword slept in its scabbard. Then he further said:

"You could go to your village back after doing what I said and lead a lavish life with your family. You need not to work here anymore. And if you negate my demand, your coffin will be made now here itself. Decide it right now."

Feared on his temper and seeing the mighty sword, he said in trembling voice:

"Yes my lord, I will heed to you"

Heera smiled and said:

"This pack of money will rest here until you do it when I demand. Heera picked up another bundle wrapped in a sack, handed to him over:

"Take it along with you and hide it somewhere within your reach without letting your colleagues know it. Now rush back with this before they come back to your camp. Don't be afraid. You will be safe, it is my word."

The man went back.

It was a day which began to close its shutters of lights and followed by a no-moon night. It was thick and dark, without even the stars twinkling in the cloudy sky above. Everybody in Bali went to sleep after their supper except the assigned guards along with Gori and Mitu keeping the vigil. Gori sensed that day something false in the movements across the borders. So she wanted Mitu stay with her at night in addition to the tower guards. When the dogs began to bark, Gori signaled Mitu and the guards to be alert. Movements heard near the entry way and whispers of men.

"Hold on!"

Cried Gori aloud and said:

"Whoever you are the cowards, sneaking in night like thieves, go back at once!"

"Proceed forward, and attack the bastards" shouted Heera outside the gate.

"Oh! You beasts of Likha, come; come, and have it if you dare!" She shot back.

The fighters about sixty tried to enter and diverse their entrance on both passages of the wall and the false fencing in haste. Swords, spears, holding in their hands in attacking gestures rushed forward through the passages. Gori signaled a whistle. Mitu, the guards and she suddenly took their arrows with metallic tips and shot them towards the fencing aiming at the stone pillars. Almost all the men excluding the last five or six men with Heera were yet to enter. The arrows flicked on the stone pillars and sparks of fire blazed which spread swiftly on the entire fencing and they were garnished with the gunpowder all along.

A wall of fire formed in a moment and the bamboos blasted within with terrible sounds and the tiny shells of stones, nails and bamboo splits scattered like fire spitting arrows. Mayhem, screams, panic appeals and shoutings....

Heera stunned in seeing this and ran back along with his few men who were stayed near the gate. The rest suffered the burns of fire and strike of stone chips, nails and the bamboo splits with its burning tips and ran around towards in and outside of Bali village screaming for help...those who sprinted inwards were encountered by the fierce dogs forcing them to back outwards but remained trapped inside helpless due to the spread of fire and fell down helpless in the filed.

Gori and her men got down from their positions and observed the injured encroachers with straw torches lighted from the fire.

"What a pity fate of the 'great knights'! Thphooo!!"

She spited on their faces and yelled:

"Go! Go away to your boss and ask him rescue. Oh how can he? He had run away with his life abandoning you fools! What a leading fighter! Fearful cowards saying them fighters!! Sneaking at night like thieves to fight! Shame on you being called as warriors!! Struggle, or die where you lie... Tomorrow our men and the dogs will have a delightful feast for their eyes."

She again spitted on the ground with utmost hate. Meanwhile, the villagers who were in deep sleep were awakened due to the sounds of blasting of bamboos and screaming of the victims gathered around there. Knowing the happenings, they were overwhelmed in the surprise of another thumping victory over the Dhirs and began to dance. They began to praise Gori and Mitu for their glorious achievement and lifted them in delight and jubilation. Gori was irritated and shouted:

"Stop this! Don't be so excited. The enemy is not so weak. They will resort to any modes of actions to conquer us. So keep these prisoners of us till morning and leave only after all of our men have a glare on them. It will raise their confidence." Then she and Mitu went to their own homes and rested.

# CHAPTER

**F**ailures after failures…

Heera was frustrated again after that night's unexpected setback. Sixteen of his men lost again in that disastrous night. His men in the village were angry over him for the foolish attack in the night. Some of them even praised in open the outstanding courage and brilliance shown by the young girl and her marginal and poor experienced fellows. They even mentioned about her parenthood linked with Heera. This further increased the anger in Heera.

He summoned the man whom he made the deal in his house earlier. When he came he said:

"Do your work as I said day after tomorrow. You just send the catchers to me when they came with the catch to your camp. I will engage them with me for enough the time you need to stuff the fishes with what I given to you. I will send to you my man to find if you finished and you just signal him. Then you come here to take your fortune from me and go straight to your village. The sellers will do the rest."

The man went back in consent.

The fish sellers visited with fish catches almost every day. Gori was unaware of the matter till the day after the night of conflict as she was used to be with the Baba at evenings for his sessions. Since fish eating was a routine habit of

Adhirs, nobody, even the guards did not felt it necessary to be a thing of significance to report to her.

She was informed by Mitu about this. She enquired

"Where from they come?"

"They are from Garu village. But the fishes were cached from the pond in Likha."

"How do you know it?"

"I spotted them yesterday and enquired."

"Does their head know this?"

"They said they don't know as they catch them in hide"

"It smells of some foul. Forbid them to sell fish here anymore."

"Why Gori, what's the matter?"

"Just do what I say." She said with firm tones.

Mitu was irritated. This habit of her always brought anger in him. After his plea for love was rejected he sometimes thought to seek to defame her at any cost. He was so much in thirst for her love. When she turned back his plea for love, he felt insulted and dejected. He was two years elder than her. But she spoke to him like a commandant, always authoritatively. It was humiliating enough. So he decided to disobey her latest order. He kept silent about the ban to sell fish and ignored her whip.

The next day came. Mitu saw the fishermen came with their catches. He thought about the ban. But a rethought born within him. If she ever knew about his disobedience, it will be unfortunate or may be even tragic to him. A terror trembled within his heart and he went speedily towards the sellers and blocked their way:

"Stop, you are banned to sell fishes here. Go back."

"My good Lord, please don't put us in hunger. Let's do this for the sake of our bellies and hungry Childs"

"No. This is a decree from the head of the village. Go away straight"

He said and soon realized in mind that how a lie slipped out of his tongue! His father was the head and he never been aware of the ban. But he cooled himself and stared at them in anger.

Then the men fell into his feet and plead for kindness. He felt a sudden kindness in mind and said:

"Alright, you can sell this catch today as it will be wasteful your hard work in the pond. But look, don't come here over again with fishes. You will be punished. Now rush and go back quickly after selling your stuff."

"Thanks a lot for your kindness to our hungry bellies, my Lord." They went in haste with their catches to the households. They went back with what they earned with expedited feet.

Soon after the sellers gone, the dogs began to moan in pain and fell dead in those households who bought fish. It was used to give tiny fishes to every dog to calm them by the sellers. Some women spotted this when they came out after fixing the vessels to the oven for cooking. They began to cry and call their men seeing their pets lay dead. The cries heard from almost every households and Mitu was the first to hear it. He enquired and when learnt, felt horrified.

"Poisoned!"

He cried aloud and ran to every household to inform and restrict the villagers from eating the fish dish. However when he managed to spread the message throughout Bali, almost all the dogs dead and some children and women or men who tasted their dishes were reported struggling to die in poisoning. The village head and his family except Mitu were amongst them.

Gori rushed to Baba and appealed him to do his best to rescue the poisoned. Baba said he was helpless in this matter, but he tried to save their lives with his herbal medicines. The poison applied was very severe in nature.

Grief and fear gripped the village. Scores of dead bodies of children, women and men and dogs piled as the black ship of death anchored in Bali to fish out human lives from that newborn village.

It lost its Headman along with the others and their sincere and charming sentinels, the dogs. Their first experience ever in their folk's history to become masters of any possession was met with a tragic end. And the first ever pride to have a man to head within from their own class. All ended in a day.

Gori had a mere assumption that Mitu evaded his responsibility. But she did not quiz him. He has lost his entire family. He tried his best to correct the mistake sincerely at last and thus clear elimination of Adhirs from the face of earth was avoided. She arranged for the burial of the corps and Baba performed the rituals as appealed by the villagers.

Villagers asked Baba to appoint a new head. Baba looked towards Mitu and said

"He will head you"

He declined.

"No Baba, I can't. Gori is the fittest. Please make her the head."

All of them agreed and urged her to accept the offer. She gave her consent with a silent nod.

Mitu meanwhile was realizing that how a mere slip of his tongue turned in to reality. Gori became the Head of the village a he predicted!

# CHAPTER

The grief and sorrows melt within the rolling wheels of time. It came the season of harvest. Fields of Likha village were the first to reap their crops. They got it in plenty. Their experience to look after the crops were much advanced and mature due to the knowledge imparted through the ancient heritage. They harvested the crops and stored them and sold the excess stocks.

Bali lagged far behind to Likha in every aspect of the cropping; in timing, growing, feeding and in its harvesting. Their out turns from the fields were very little. Poor tilling, feeding, irrigation or clearing of pests and reaping were improper. Even though, they got enough to store for their upcoming months.

The harvests were over. Heera maintained some calm after the poison episode. He was busy with the crops and its maintenances. Manab almost become a priest and rarely did he go home. Always devoted to prayers and reciting the scriptures within the priest's room.

Beera is expected to come back soon after his studies with the other boys of the village sent along with him to Garu. Heera did not have any hints of the whereabouts of his absconding wife and companion. He did not give up the quest so far and tried to gather information on them by all means while planning another attack on the Adhirs to wipe them out of the village of Bali. His mind thrived to dominate the entire Likhabali as it was in its vastness and fertility earlier. His mind never conceded the division.

There were two hearts burning in quest of wild revenge. Their eyes could not embrace sleep in nights; brains could not stay paused in anything, and their minds hurting with ever fuming burns of the sudden defeat.

Those were the hearts of Gori and Mitu.

It was quite natural for Gori by her nature. But the soft minded Mitu became more rigid and rough after the carnage. He stayed in solitude almost in his leisure time. He was very keen on each session of training especially in swords. He inspired his subordinates to excel. He always enquired with Gori only about the time and scheme of their plan of revenge. Their army of men was being prepared for a bitter and crucial conflict.

Soon after Gori chosen as the Head after the carnage unanimously, she pledged to revenge at the very earliest. Baba called her in one evening and said

"Daughter, it is bleeding very much on both sides. Killing is not the single mean to achieve peace. There are other ways left to us by God."

"Baba, do you think that the 'other ways' we seek could help us to win Heera over? And can we easily forget the drastic death of our beloved people and the innocent pets? We are not after them to dominate but they does not leave us to our fates."

"Yes, Heera is such a beast that there are no alternatives we could look into. But the bleeding is in excess. You must keep it in mind"

"Yes Baba, I know it. We will look into it after his burial. There will be no peace if Heera is alive."

Baba lost in thought and retired to his room. He then called Mitu another day, then said to him

"Son, I know that you all are preparing some drastic in revenge"

"Yes Baba, we think it is our bonded duty"

"Then you must give me a word of promise"

"Ask anything Baba, I will do it out of any hesitation"

"Not so much. Only one thing: do not let Heera be killed by Gori. Patricide is sinful. You know that. If it happens it will burn her throughout the whole life. So I ask you to do the needful at the right time when it comes there an encounter between them"

"Baba, I give you my word that I will not let her do it. From this very moment, Heera is my own prey. I will not spare him to anybody"

With strong determination, he went back. He will not let anybody snatch away his prey from his mouth. If it happens so, he will kill the snatcher first and then the prey.

'The bastard killed my dear parents....and my beloved folk mates. He deserves its befitting reply..." Mitu resolved.

It was the end of spring. Cuckoos called here and there with sweet songs. It trumpeted the call for celebration and performance of the annual offerings.

People of Likha were engaged to celebrate their annual ritual of traditional offerings to the serpents, their re-incarnated forefathers. Every household were washed with water. The streets were swept to clean and were decorated to give the village in a festive look.

The Dhirs were very strict in observing and practicing the traditional rituals. The villagers specially the male members below sixty years should fast all the day till the end of the chanting of the sacred manthras in night. They offered milk, ghee and sweets to the snakes and their deity and performed various rituals praying for their grace and benevolences. After the sacred functions, they made community feasts at the vast tent house near the shrine of their deity.

During this period of a week, they were asked to abstain from any kinds of wrongdoings. They could not carry arms; they should remain calm with pleasant thoughts and they could not use any words of curses, abuses or reprimands. Should always wear clean cloths, bath thrice daily before the rituals, in the morning, noon and at evenings.

Heera ran around the village to invite every member to attend the function as he was duty bound to do so being as the head of Likha village. He had in mind a fear of the strike back from the Adhirs. So he engaged the fighters brought from outside to keep guard on the village. He also instructed his own men to keep vigil and keep their arms at their reach. He said that if the occasion demands so they should pick up the weapons and reciprocate directly without considering the rituals and its rules of traditions. He was aware and concerned of the brilliance and shrewdness of Gori, his own blood. She could attack Likha, at any moment...

"The gift of God"
Said Mitu in happiness spilled over within his heart.
"The ripe time is this" he uttered in delight.
"Plan us our scheme of attack and it's the apt time" said Gori.

They gathered; all the one hundred and fifty of their fighters, in the evening. The leaders of every gang came forward. All sat in line. Gori and Mitu detailed their plan of actions alternatively, touching every aspect of the procession. The members told to ask any doubts or suggestions. They cleared and accepted every of the decisions felt logical and helpful. Gori and Mithu alternately motivated them with cordial chats and finally everybody took oath of the adherence to the mission and vowed to win at any cost and disbursed to march at their stipulated time schedule.

The day before the final functions; every men member of Likha were required to participate in unison to offer the apologetic rituals to their deity and serpents for their wrongdoings, mistakes or sinful actions in the past. Various priests lead the rituals and asked them to follow their directions. Elders, ladies, girls and children glaring them on and repeating the rites in their minds as the custom demanded. Almost the entire village was camped in the tent house. The long function went on and on towards night...

The tent was shook by sudden and loud war-cry and every occupant of the tent stood and looked outwards. They saw armed fighters in their spree of violent advancements from all sides of the tent. With arrows and bows, swords swung in swiftness with thirst of blood and flesh, spears sharpened to strike through targets, loud calls from the gang leaders for attack... women, children and old aged were trembled and screamed for help, the guards tried to defend in vain, the Adhir fighters were on their high spirits to thrash and harm and kill anybody got in the reach of their arms.

Heera ordered his men to take arms but they were too trembled and failed to gather their arms in the sudden surprise and mayhem created by the Adhirs. He himself took out his sword and began to fight back. He alone could not do much. Many of his men killed or hurt and some of them ran away looking in search of their kith and kin to save their lives. Women and children became panic in helplessness and pleaded for pardon in the feet of their enemies.

Gori targeted Heera with his swords. She was without shields, so was her habit. Heera fought back with his mighty sword and shield. Fierce fighting went on. Sparks of fires flicked out of swords...Fight of father and daughter seeking to kill each other. She jumped up when an attacking swing sword came from Heera and thrashed a kick in his bare head with her feet and he fell down imbalanced. She tossed away his sword and got him at the point of her sword. As he tried to get up to his feet, she raised her sword upwards with all her strength to behead him but in a moment, a flying spear came suddenly and struck in the breast of Heera and a shout from Mitu stopped her.

"No Gori, it's your father. Let me have him, that beast is mine"

He shot an arrow from his bow after the spear. Heera fell down bearing the spear in his chest with the fatal arrow stuck in body and eventually, his end of life was inevitable... Meanwhile, a spear struck Mitu from his back sent by one of Heera's guards and he also fell down in the tent.

With loud yelling and sparkling eyes, Gori went through out the tent and its surroundings unleashing a terrible and fierce attack. She killed so many and destroyed what she met with...Bloody bodies scattered all along within the tent. Gori got red from head to her toes.. bleeding from the inflicted injuries on her body and face...she called aloud to eliminate all the men...

There were not much left to confront... painful moans and screams...of children, women and injured... when she realized that the enemy were nowhere, she called her men to lift the body of her own men dead or seriously injured... and with them they returned to Bali, jubilant and content with the absolute victory over the enemy. The Adhir men went on their way by ransacking, looting and spreading destructions throughout Likha village. Gori did not try to restrict or stop them...

# CHAPTER

**D**uring all these course of happenings, Manab was sitting meditated in the priest room. He did not ever come out as he was fully immersed in deep prayer, like ancient yogis, absolutely unattached to the living world...

Gori went straight to Baba's hut as her followers began to celebrate their superior victory. She could not find Baba there in his seat but the cloth bundle bearing some scriptures in palm leave laid there and a message scripted afresh left on his seat said to her:

**"Going back to the hills, seek peace in re-union and love"**

She stood there, like a statue, posed as holding the crown of victory in one of her hand and the bouquet of gratitude in the other, longing to offer in those deserving feet of Baba. And he is no more there to receive....

He had gone, leaving her orphan.

Two drops of tears fell in to the very piece of palm leaf bearing the message, shone like those shining eyes of Baba looking into her face with affection. Her heart swelled with despair like child's... She sat in her knees down leaning to the empty seat and begun to weep... She wept to cry. Tears shed like a sudden flow from the outbreak of a hilltop...

Tears of joy of the elimination of her enemy, tears of satisfaction to have total revenge, tears of sorrow over the loss of her fellow folks in the carnage, tears of humiliation borne out by her inability to rescue Mitu, tears of terrible pain being she left orphaned by her beloved Baba and at last the tears of regression came out of the guilt by the sinful assassination of her genetic father....

She cried like a child lying there and the tears formed a flood within the hut like they could not find exits to flow out in confusion whether to leave her alone.... She cried till the last drop of tear poured out from the lake of her captivity in the inner self.... Then she felt weightless. She is now floating over the flood of tears for a while and at last, she immersed into its deepness asleep....

# PART 2

# CHAPTER

*I love hunger,*
*For it worth grain a tiny*
*I love thirst,*
*For it dreamt a dew of honey*
*I love tiresome,*
*For it drives to do any*
*I love hatred,*
*For it tempt to love so many*
*Come love on,*
*For us dance in many and many...*

# CHAPTER

## 14

The next day, after the tragic conflict, a group of youngsters arrived in Likha lead by Beera. They were about twenty, returned to their homely village after their studies and trainings at Garu.

They were informed of the tragic episode met to their folks on their way to home itself. Before getting into his home, Beera went along with his friends to the priest's seat to offer prayers and seek the graces of the deity along with others. There he met his father who sat in his meditation. After offering the rituals he called him. Then he opened his eyes and called him nearby his seat and whispered him something private. Then he graced all of them.

A terribly silenced Likha welcomed them with mutilated dead bodies begun to decay, injured men and women and woeful residents looted and assaulted. Cows, goats and buffalos strayed in the streets and fields in search of their masters...

Beera surveyed whole Likha village with his company. Visited every household and tried to sooth and console the grieving villagers. He consulted the remained elders in the village about the urgent need of clearing debris and burials of the dead. They all approved and extended their helping hands to him.

Beera assumed as the head of Likha at the pressing demand and wish of the villagers. His mother also encouraged him to take over but advised him to be fair and just in his delivery of duties.

He was sitting in his chair the next morning he assigned as the Head of the Likha. He picked the tumbler of milk his mother served. His men were outside chatting each other. Then the gate thrashed to open. A gang of about fifteen men rushed in through the open gate lead by a young lady in arms. Her face and body covered in cloths of red. She stormed in haste in to the house in violent gestures and enquired where Beera is. The men chatted outside got up quick to defense with swift pick of spears in their arms. They made a blockade with their arms and denied access.

Beera saw it and shouted from his seat aloud

"Let her come inside, keep the others there itself"

They allowed the girl who was in fumes of fury and they gazed her sprinting inside.

"Welcome you my sweetness. Come, sit please"

"Have the sweetness of death from this bitter sword"

She cried in wrath with blazing looks from her sun like eyes and she straightly began to attack him with the sword. Beera did not get up, just picked up a belt rolled around his hip. He unlocked it with a push of his thump and the belt further unrolled to double its length and he began to swing it around over his body. It was a metal plate wide about the length of his palm and four feet long and weighty but very flexible. With the speedy swinging, it made a virtual round shield.

Beera swung it around with the left hand and continued to defend with ease and high flexibility while drinking the milk with his right hand. He just concentrated in the movements of her feet downwards and swung his belt in tune with her footsteps. Blazes of fire sparkled spontaneously with the clashes of the belt with her swift movements of the lengthy sword...

She swung her sword all around him with increased zeal but he continued to defend and completed his drink of milk without letting down a drop to her wonder and astonishment. Then he stood up in a while and jumped over to her back, turned and trapped her in a knot of his right hand and the belt!

She became a statue losing her nerves and breath with a finger of his hand pressed somewhere behind her back and her sword fell down with a sound of flicking on the floor.

He grasped her from back and loosed the trap a little in her relief and whispered with the warm breath which burned her back of neck:

"Love; love is the only weapon mightiest in the world. I will win you over with that"

The soft and emotional words fell into her ears which made a vibrant spark throughout her entire body. She held the head down and tried to release from him in vain.

"Leave me"

She said slowly with a trembling voice, sad and shame gripping her throat.

Meanwhile the gang accompanied her were also trapped outside. There were only ten men outside the house. The encroachers were of fifteen. In a tackling move the ten men divided into five groups and encountered with three at a time and they trapped within their two spears each three of them captive in five traps. Nobody fought back but just defended and not a single scratch made on anybody.

He freed her. She went out rushing and calling her companions.

"Free them and let them go with her in due honors"

Beera ordered aloud with a smile and continued to her:

"You fought with great excellence. Congratulations! We will meet again"

That was he, Beera; handsome in looks, bright in brain and great in wisdom. Filled with a heart of compassion; he was simple, humble and sensitive but have peerless valor.

The others present in the house became mute spectators in wonder.

"Why did you let them go free, son" one elder enquired, irritated.

"They deserve freedom" Beera said and smiled.

"They are the slaughters of your uncle and a lot of our beloved. They looted us and cruelly hurtled our fighters. It is unfair to free them but should have been killed here itself so that the departed souls of our beloved men could be relieved in heaven."

Said another elder man, whose expressions showed disgust and he continued:

"A golden opportunity has been wasted"

Beera smiled and looked towards his mother gently.

"What you do think about it mother, please"

"Do what your conscience commands. I have nothing more to say"

"That is what I am doing and going to continue with. Time will prove its worth. Thank you mother"

He stood up and prepared to go out.

"Where, son, are you going?" Mother asked.

"I am going to the farm fields. I will be late. Please don't wait for me for the lunch" he exited with his group.

Beera took a wide look on the fields which was lying waste with the grass and pests grown wild to make the farming tough and expensive. It got too late to initiate the cropping. He engaged some men under his command to clear up the fields and to begin the farming proceedings.

He was fond of farming. He loves plants, trees and flowers. Cattles were his pet. He restricted his fellow men not to hurt birds and flies. A man filled with love for every creature in the nature. The fields were vast and spread that he came back his home very late in the evening tired.

On her return, Gori went straight to her own home with a face of shame and despair. Her men already got the news of their experience at Likha. They asked her a lot of questions to which she kept silence and hurried towards her room. The humiliation was unbearable. She fell down in her bed and wept. It was the first defeat in her life as a fighter. That too without being fought back! Trapped and captured by a few defending men. Her sadness slowly meltdown in the wonderful thought that such tactics exist in combats! Keenness budded in her heart and she thought about the actions of her opponents.

And then the words he spelt to her suddenly emerged in her mind,

'Love'

It again made a flint of spark in her. 'Love!' what is it feels like?' she was puzzled a lot to think about it.

'No, it is not for me to think so silly passions' she tried to assert in mind and tried to deflect her thoughts.

'It is usual in fights to be defeated. Temporary setbacks, that's all this. I will overcome this trivial' she thought aloud to console herself but, in vain. The pictures of her and her men's captivity disturbed her further. She tried to sleep. Her longings for sleep besides the tiredness did not bore any fruit.

'If I would have been there with more men in spite of those fifteen the result would have been different' another consolation... She was perplexed in such various thoughts and soothing excuses during that whole day and night.

# CHAPTER

15

'What a girl she is! So daring to attack a village with the few men trained within too short a period. They fought with the skills of greatest warriors. And she doesn't hold a shield. Dire intend to attack. Not ever concerned to protect her self. The trainer who made these ignorant people into this sort of fighters must have great caliber and wisdom'

Beera was so impressed about his opponents despite the fact that they had fully destructed his own village and almost eliminated most of its men.

He could not remember her face. Only the blazing eyes spitting fire were in his recall. A desire budded in him to see her once more. He deflected from his thoughts when a fellow of him brought a man in. It was a resident of Likha. He welcomed him to sit and asked

"How are you? What prompted you to here?"

"My lord, I keep goats. It strays into the fields now lying barren. Some times when I leave them in urgency, they used to graze throughout the fields belong to the Adhirs. When any Adhirs notice it they drive them to their homes and keeps there. When I went to bring back they denies and abuses me with threats of assault. Today they have kept my eight goats. Now they have fifteen goats of mine with them. I am a poor, living hand to mouth with the mere earnings comes out of my sheep. I pray Your Lord; please help to bring my goats back"

"Today you went there?'

"Yes My lord"

"Who is the man who kept your sheep?"

"Litta, who resides in the east end corner near the farm fields?"

"Please stay with us; I will try to bring them back"

The man went back and sat on the veranda with an unpleasant face. He was not sure that he will get his sheep back considering the past disastrous encounters of Likha men with the Adhirs. But a ray of hope remained in his mind with the news of the latest encounter at Likha. He heard that Bali's men had a bitter experience with Beera.

'This youngster may help me but the Adhirs became too strong a folk now to defeat'

He thought in mind.

Beera was in search to find a pretext to get into Bali. He desired badly to meet her and have a glare on her face and to converse freely. So he proceeded to Bali with two of his fellows and the goat keeper. When he reached the entrance, the guard came to him.

"I want to meet your Head. Please go and bring her permission if it is granted"

The guard was stunned to hear such gentle words from a young man of the elite class. The first enemy visitor came ever to this new village with a request to meet its head.

"Alright My lord, please stay here. I will be back right now"

Then he rushed towards Gori's home near there.

Beera glanced at the village and its households. He noticed the changes. Baba made it! Clean pathways and the surroundings around homes, well thatched roofs and newly planted trees and growing gardens came in his sight with delight.

'Baba's magic!'

He assumed with a little wonder. The old memories of dirty roads and houses came into his mind with some guilt. The guilt came out from the brutality exerted on Adhirs by his ancestors. They forced Adhirs to live in pitifully denying all humanly privileges. The guilt came out from the unforgivable sins committed against the sacred scripts and its intensions.

Then he looked towards the area outside the entrance where there was existed the large banyan tree for past many years. There were a shadow of its shades and it was cool and fresh and he used to sit beneath it with his friends and played in childhood. Now there he spotted two thin siblings growing separately without having any contacts and relationships to each other but they fed through one and only root stem existed beneath them.

The guard said to Gori.

"One young man, with two fellows is asking to meet you. They are from Likha"

"Are they in arms?"

"No. One of them holds a small bag. Nothing else"

Gori paused in thought.

'It would be he; Beera the new head.'

During her lessons, she were taught to welcome any visitors coming to village be treated as hosts and due respect would be provided, by the Baba.

"Bring them in with due respect"

The guard went back and she withdrew to her room.

When Beera came to Gori's house premises, 'My lord' the dog which was survived the carnage with a few others, barked aloud and went aggressively towards them.

"My lord, keep quiet, I am your friend."

Beera said calmly and he placed the pieces of bread he brought with him in a bag. The dog suddenly went calm and began to sniff his feet and ran around him pleasantly swinging its tails in gratitude. They become friends and Beera played with him for a while and looked towards the door of the house. Seeing the visitors, Gori's parents exited and came to him

"My lord, you came into this mere hut of ours!"

They exclaimed and offered their respects. They knew him since his childhood and liked him very much with his charming behavior. He was so kind and loving to the villagers in his childhood.

"I want to see the head of your village. Is she your daughter, Gori?" He asked. He had seen them in childhood some one or two times and knows their names. He was restricted then to mingle or play with the Childs of Adhirs by his elders, especially by his uncle Heera.

"Yes my Lord, please be seated."

They said and called the others came with him to sit in a bench lied on the veranda. Gori's father further called turning towards the inner room.

"Gori, come, and look who's the Great Lord, stepped into our home!"

Gori was kept inside herself after a look at him through the window in bewilderment. She was puzzled a bit. 'What should I do with them?' she thought.

She made her mind to meet him and exited.

"What do you want?"

With a tone of abruptness, she asked.

"Good evening" Beera said.

He looked towards the voice and remained still. He felt a breeze swinging around there and darkness spread in while and from within, a full moon rose before him pouring around there a kind of pleasant fragrance of brightness. She offered a smile. A smile like a spring was leashed within her beautiful lips...

He felt flying in the marvelous wings of love up above the empty infinite heights

He felt got oysters within his hold brought from the bluish depths the ocean of love

He felt captured in his fists the greener pastures of oasis from the deserts of love....

"My lord, please take your seat." Gori's father said mildy.

Beera suddenly came back to his normal senses. He released himself from the sudden astonishment on her sight and replied, "Yes".

Beera sat in the seat and asked his men to sit with him. Then Gori asked.

"Please tell us what do you want with us now?"

"I came to you with a minor problem. Let us go to the Baba's hut so as I can have a look at it and have a word with you about my issue"

She gestured in positive and led him towards the hut. She did not visit the hut since the day Baba went back leaving the message. The three men accompanied Beera also followed them. All were kept silence till they reached Baba's hut.

Beera went towards the empty seat of Baba and bowed in his knees paying respects. When he bowed down, his eyes stuck on a piece of scripted palm leaf lying beneath him. It seems to be lying there for many a days. He read it in a while and stood up staring at Gori.

She was silently observing all his actions in wonder. She cannot believe that this man carries the same blood that Heera carried in his veins. What a contradiction!

Beera smiled suppressing something he indented to say.

"Please be seated and come to the point. Don't try to tease us" Gori said.

"Alright, the problem is very silly. One of our poor village men is living with his sheep. Unfortunately some of his sheep, about fifteen, were forcefully kept by somebody named Litta who resides near the farms at the east end corner of your village. I need your help to get them back."

"I do not know about this sheep affair. But it is sure that no one from Bali village ever crosses over to your area. The sheep might trespass in to Litta's fields. So he might keep them bound. It is not his fault."

"Animals do not trespass but browse in pastures to feed themselves; it is man who does encroach or trespass. I am not blaming Litta for holding the sheep. But when its keeper approached, he faulted by threatening and inclining to give it back"

Gori thought for a while and said:

"You came here to complain about a mere crime committed by an ignorant man...

She paused for a moment and continued:

"Have you ever thought about the innumerable crimes and brutalities committed on us in the past?"

"I am fully aware and so much ashamed of it. I cannot justify those sins with mere an apology or regret. Now the question is whether wrongs could be corrected by reciprocating with another wrong. I don't believe so. As far as I am concerned, I can assure you that nothing objectionable to you will be done from our side so long as I am there. I also can assure you about my fellows too. But it is difficult to change the mindset of the elders. I am in that effort to change them and it will take a long time. I request your help in my attempts, so that we could have a peaceful co-existence"

She was listening to him patiently. His mild and sweat words emitted directly from a kind heart. His words of conviction touched her. She asked

"What is there I could help you with?"

"You may advice your men to abstain from any misdeeds to Likha's men so as the elders got an excuse to act me on you. It will inflict injuries on my efforts to change their mindset"

Gori send a guard of her to summon Litta along with the captured sheep. As they come, she said to Litta.

"Do not ever try to indulge in this kind of actions. You thieved the robbers. Go back leaving the sheep here. If anything comes to your fields, just drive them out. We are not thieves or beggars. We could live with our own hardships."

Litta went back with a rough and unpleasant face. He was disappointed over the decision of his village head. He was planning to sell the sheep to the merchant for a good sum; a sum which he never earned in his entire life. Now all those dreams got in vain. But it is an order which he could not defy.

She said then to Beera

"Your man could have his sheep back"

Beera smiled on her comments and said "thank you, now one of the business is over

"Is there anything else?"

"Yes, a personal one"

Saying this he hinted towards the others and they went out to count the sheep.

"You have still another problem with us?" She asked.

"Yes, with some one here"

"How is and what is it?"

"I have a problem with beautiful and marvelous things. It fills insanity to my head. I want to be healed."

A glimpse of smile glazed on her face which was looking downwards. She said.

"The Baba was our healer. He is no more here."

"I saw him in his seat when I bowed there. He whispered the remedy in my ears and left a prescription"

"Where is it?"

He showed the palm leaf lying there. With a tiny shock, she picked it and said

"It meant to me."

"It meant to both of us... and I love you very much"

He said and went out asking the fellows to take along the sheep. Gori kept stayed there with a passion she could not identify. She wondered how this Dhir man had studied about Bali and its proceedings. He was out of the village for so long a time. How did he gather so much information about us? She wondered.

'He is different. He is genuine and he is lovely! Oh! What is happening in me? I am not after love. Such waste sentiments should be kept out of the doors of my mind.' she mused and got out of the hut. But the scripture reminded something other to her.

'Is love is so great?'

A cool breeze swirled in her heart. She felt the transformation forming from within. She felt rejoiced and experienced the dancing of a kind of thrill and urge to be loved.

'Baba, I am in love. I could not bear without love.'

Her legs, stepping throughout towards her home were longing to dance in that beautiful evening in sequence to her delightful musings...

# CHAPTER

**16**

The farms got ready to have conceived with the seasonal crops. Farmers of both the villages started this time almost in the same period. But some fields of the Adhirs were left aside due to the lack of cattle to plough them. It was noticed by Beera. He asked his men to lend some of their cattle to Adhirs. Nobody paid any heed. He cannot compel them to do so because the cattle are their personal holdings. But he himself owned a lot. So he along with the willing fellow men decided to provide them to Adhirs. The farming Adhirs were very happy to receive these helping gestures with gratitude.

What so ever were the fates occurred to the Dhirs after the division, there were one folk which remained there in silence and unbothered; the snakes. They were in plenty and happy with the Dhirs. They were treated and kept well. Those creeping creatures were given due respect and well offered care.

But on the contrary, Adhirs were envying them so far as earlier for the snakes still enjoyed high privilege in Likha.

So the Adhirs did not show any mercy on them even after the division. They rampantly killed every snake spotted on their soil and burned their eggs when found anywhere. It was a thought thoroughly drilled in their mind that a snake is a creature to be killed at sight. They used to do it even in the earlier in hiding when the undivided Likhabali was in existence and in open now at Bali.

So there became another creature, the rat, began breeding to multiple their numbers in huge and plenty. The village filled with mouse and rats crawling here and there day and night. Villagers noticed the growth of rats and were disturbed a lot but helpless to control. Some of the Adhirs have had delightful dish out the huge rats when they got to have killed them.

Most of the men among Dhirs and the Adhirs were satisfied with the actions of their new heads leading their respective villages. After all the peace is coming in sight and a cool life could be lead without any fear. Most of them relieved. But there were resentments too.

Shila was living with the Dhirs happily. She was regularly visited by Heera for his sexual urges and rewarded her hands filled. Some other fighters were often visited her. She was even provided the girls who were kept in touch with her secretly to the men who needed and made a bit of fortune out of them. With Gori and Beera being the heads, she also faced troubles in Likha.

As said earlier, there were a few who were in dissent. Some of the elders disliked Beera for his magnanimity for freeing Gori with her captive men, disapproved his visit to Bali for the sheep with request and his plea for lending the cattle. They were murmuring dissent in their own groups and cursed him privately. The families of the men whose genitals chopped out were also in great revolt.

Manik, who was a spy planted by the Maji village head was unhappy towards Gori over the sheep episode. Littu angrily said when he met Manik:

"Gori cheated us. She ordered to give back the sheep of those scoundrels. I was thinking to sell my catches of sheep to you. But that new lad in Likha and Gori spoiled all my expectations."

"You are right Litta, something should be done. I will think over it."

In his next trip to Maji to procure his trading goods, he visited Danab, his master and village head as usual. Manik apprised him of every detail of happenings in Bali and Likha. Danab thought for a while and said:

"Don't worry. What is going on is graceful to me. You just keep in touch with the dissidents and try to encourage more to dissent. Keep the men among the Dhirs in contact and try instigating against Beera. Be careful, he is a brilliant lad. Always be careful."

"Yes My Lord. I will keep you updated."

"You must meet me before you go back."

When he met Danab before his departure, Danab introduced three men to Manik and said.

"These are my men. You take along them to Bali with you and arrange to settle them there. They will help you better in our plans."

"Yes my lord."

He came back to Bali with his goods and the three men. He went on with his actions in secret to increase the dissent amongst both the villagers during the course of his trading.

Harmony prevailed among Bali and Likha. Life went on normally but turmoil was forming within the bottom which was unseen. Beera got some tips through his faithful fellows. He asked them to gather more evidence and information from both sides.

Beera was in unrest of mind. He did not meet Gori after the sheep episode. It is not fair to go to Bali without a valid reason. So he was in search of one.

On the other part, Gori was also looking keen to meet him at any of the pretext. Her heart longed for him and to converse more and more about nothing but their selves. Every night was filled with his thoughts. Every day, she sought his face in every incomer passing through the entrance.

The three men came with Manik were gamblers. They also were expert in brewing. They made wines from grains after processing them with some herbs. When in leisure time the three men sat outside the shop of Manik and began to play their cards. They bet money with every game. In every game some of them wins and grab all the money they bade.

Villagers of Bali often used to sit beside them and looked on the gambling curiously. They saw how money is made within seconds with a pack of cards. The losers did not ever grieve before them but consoled them self saying:

"I will win the next."

Then they continued to play to generate interest in the on looking villagers as per their pre conceived plan.

Some of the Adhirs asked them to teach them to play cards. The Maji men were happy to impart their gambling expertise to them and they sat for hours and played with them. The new players were happy enough that they got money every day. They were served with the wine brewed and enjoyed it gradually. Thus the number of gamblers grew to large numbers.

The homes belong to the playing men become disturbed in unrest and violence. They were happy when they got unexpected money but it was often. Drunken Adhirs beat their women and children when they complained. The habit of playing cards gradually gripped more and more with the intake of wine.

Likha also came into the gradual grasp of wine and cards. In Likha, Shila's home was the camp of Maji men. They attracted several youths and men to their folds. Lured to the easy money and the delight of wine, youngsters and men forgot to work.

One day, a woman complained Beera with tears of frustration that her young son was trapped in his new habits of drink and cards. He used to steal money from home and spent on wines and even used to stay in their playing camp for days. When he came back to home he used to be seen offended and aggressive to other members of the family. So she wants his urgent help to bring back his son on the right track. Beera was touched by her tears and words of grief. He assured her to do the needful at his earliest.

Beera called his fellow entrusted with the task of gathering information on the anti social activities. He reported him in details what he gathered so far. He briefed about the three new out comers from Maji and about their deeds. Beera got hints about the plans of Danab could have plotted against his village.

He decided to visit Bali first to tackle the issue to draft out a joint plan to deal with the new crisis. And it was a grace in disgust for him. He could meet her again!

# CHAPTER

**17**

G ori was delighted to see the scene of Beera's entrance. She treated the plants in the garden which the Baba grownup in front of the hut. Now a days, she used to spare maximum of her time spending with flowers and dreams. She got into that habit after he said those last words in the hut. Those words fuelled the refinement in her. When he was approaching, she made try to hide her emotions and expressed a formal look and said:

"What is the problem now prompted you towards this little hut"

Beera also tried to be formal.

"I am sorry. There is a serious one this time which concern you too."

"What is it?"

She said after inviting him to sit.

"Gori, something unwanted is going on in both of our villages. You may have noticed that now a day, a few newcomers settled in your village engaged themselves to attract people towards wine and gambling. This created unrest in most of the households. In my perception, they are the men planted here by our old rival Danab, the head of Maji village which is situated between Garu and ours. He is still keeping his eyes on our part of this land with bad intentions to capture and have revenge for the earlier defeat. Otherwise we do something to curb them; it will be disastrous to whole of us."

"Yes I have also noticed something abnormal. Litta who was forced by me to give away with the sheep seems unhappy with me. And there the people are gambling and drinks wine. How can we control them and what can we do with their personal affairs?"

She asked.

"So far as their habits are deemed as their personal affairs, we are helpless. But we can expel the outsiders for disturbing the social order prevailing now here. Since they are settled in Bali, I have no right to do anything about them. You are in the authority here and you could do it."

"That is right."

Then she called the guards and said to send some men in arms to bring the outsiders.

"Please let my men also go with them. Please instruct your men not to inflict any injury on them and bring them unharmed. My men could do it."

She agreed and his men accompanied the Adhir men to bring the outsiders. Then she turned to Beera and asked

"Why, they are culprits in our village and should be punished severely"

"Punishment doesn't only mean physical assault. It should be more than that to compel them to refine their mindset on actions with other fellow beings. I am against all kind of physical assaults in between humans. Violence in my view, doesn't bear any fruits except unrest in minds"

"But the world is largely subscribed to it."

"Yes, that is the tragic reality. Man resorts to own the path others shown in blind belief that it is the only means towards success. It is true that sometimes violence become unavoidable for survival. But it is a false illusion that it is the only and only road to go through."

"I cannot understand you Beera. It seems that you belong to some other world."

"But I can understand you well. Because I am not seeking to find anything wrong in you and I am not averse to negate or accept anything against me. It is not your fault that you anticipate the wrongs from me. It was your and your men's bitter experiences of the past which compels you to see us in hostility. And the same is with the Dhir men towards you. We have to try together to overcome the ills in our minds"

"Together? We have already split in two. Look Beera, look there at outside, at our boundary. There are now two banyan trees growing separately instead of the old one. How can it become one?"

She pointed her fingers towards the new born banyan trees growing up over to the boundary walls, outside.

"Gori"

He called her in a voice which was wet and mild filled with complete passion and love.

"Please have patience and trust in me. I will show you how it could be possible. I just need your loving hearts to boost up my morals. Will you give it?"

Gori looked him with her eyes wet in tears. Yes she could not deny him now.

"I will"

She said and then he come forward and grasped her within his hands. She felt lifted to the heavens and she wished to remain so for ever.

Beera kissed her in the forehead and released her from his grasp. And said

"Thank you." He kissed her hand and said again "Thank you, Gori."

Then the guards brought the three men who came from Maji. After severe questioning and interpretations, with the suggestions from Beera, Gori ordered her guards that the three of them be put in to solitary confinement for three months in the village prison of Bali. Beera went back with a satisfaction to have achieved his love and goal.

Manik came to meet Gori in the evening.

"You are ungrateful. You forget all that I have done for you to be victorious over the Dhirs."

"Why? What are you saying?" She asked.

"I have helped you to bring the stuffs of gun powder and with which you have once won over the Dhirs. Now you have put my men in prison in return. What is it but if not ingratitude?"

"Look Manik. You helped us and we provide help to smoothly settle here to do your trade. It is you doing treason by accommodating evil elements to destroy the peaceful atmosphere and lives of people prompting them towards gambling and drinking. We could not tolerate this kind of your actions ever. Keep it in your mind. If you intents to repeat, we will be forced to expel you."

The merchant stood in silence and thought something in mind and went back.

# CHAPTER

**18**

The crops were growing and got ripe to be harvested. Dhirs have got a robust crop as usual.

The Adhirs got a poor crop but their crops getting to ripe were begun to be eaten up by the rats. A large chunk of the ever multiplying rats were forced to settle themselves in the farm fields. The Adhir's kitchens were not enough filled with much grains to feed them. And Likha's sentinels were the snakes, who were looking forward for any rats dares to come even by mistake; they will have dinner with the dish for their lucky mates.

So with the grain bearing fields made heavenly stay for the rats. No more crawling, searching or wanderings for food. Just come out from the holes and have enough meals and go back to hide in the holes again. No rat eaters either the snakes or the Adhirs will hunt them at least for the time being.

The Dhirs were happy to accumulate a huge quantity of grains in their harvest. The snakes made it possible. And they prayed and vowed more offerings to them.

Rats almost entirely harvested the Adhir crops leaving a few for their masters as tips for their sweats rigorously shed on their lands.

Manab dreamt of a little girl screaming in thirst and hunger during his sleep. Suddenly he awakened from the bed and lost in thought for some time. He got some tips of that extra ordinary dream.

'Yes it is not a pleasant one. I should warn him' he thought.

In the morning, when Beera come there to offer his regular daily prayer, Manab said:

"Son, it is tough time ahead for the whole two villages. You would not sell the grains stored. Ask the others to do so. Arrange for more sources of water."

"Father, let me know what it is prompting you to say this?"

"There are some signs shown by the Almighty to warn us in advance, and I got to have that kind of one. I think a severe draught is in the pipeline which will blow an acute famine to thrust a lot of sufferings."

"Do you believe in omens?" Beera asked.

"Some phenomenon in the nature tempted me to believe so. May it be superstitious to you? It is entirely up to you to believe in such things. But what is there you are going to loss if you got prepared in advance? If it happens truly, you could face it with your well preparedness. Otherwise, there is no loss expect some efforts."

"Yes father, I will do the needful" Beera conceded.

Next morning Beera found a message but not Manab in the priest's room. The message said:

**"Good bye, don't ever seek for a priest for you. The scriptures will lead you. Learn and teach and refine them as time demands"**

The summer on Likha and Bali got to start with dry and humid weather. The sun shone every day with merciless blaze. No sign of breeze or clouds. The plants and trees began to dry up with scare of water. Animals and creatures tired, out in thirst.

Beera forbade his men the sale of grains to outsiders. He appealed to avoid wastage of edibles. He arranged to dig deep wells throughout the village to fetch water. Such wells were new to the village. He learned about it from Garu where water scared due to lack of vast ponds and used to dig deep wells finding lands consists of soft rocks.

He called the merchants and asked them to keep their carts ready with up to date repairing. Manik, the merchant left the village fearing charges of treason. He went back to Maji.

Beera conveyed to Gori about the impending draught succeeded by possible famine. He sent advisories to her and assistances to dig wells. Gori was out of carts. She asked Beera to provide to build some carts for Bali.

Even after the three men confined to their cells, people addicted to gambling continued to play. Somebody in hide while others, in open. The Adhirs were disappointed over the agricultural outcomes. Some of them decided not to venture in farming. Their hard work and dedications were returned with frustrating losses.

Disappointed, they began to gamble in search of instant and good fortunes. Even the women and children were seen trying their lucks in cards. Some gained and more of them lost their earnings and even their holdings, properties in rampant gambling.

So there formed a group of families comprising the losers constituting the bankrupted. Their numbers grew day to day. It caused a kind of anarchy and unrest in the villages. Complaints poured into the seats of village heads.

Adding fuel to the unexpected and strange phenomenon of draught, gambling and wine increased their headaches. Beera advised Gori through a message that at first they should concentrate to tackle draught seriously. The later problem can wait though it should also need to be contained.

Drought spread its tentacles. The earth began to burn in the wrath of highly fumed sun that drove away all the wet winds into far horizons away. Sun rays become shafts of fire, drilled in to the lands to inflict deep wounds of cracks everywhere. Ponds dried and its bottom floors cracked in the sun burns. All of the living beings, within and over the land become thirsty and tiresome. Birds flied, leaving the village over to away pastures. Animals and reptiles have no way left out but to remain in miseries of thirst and hunger.

But the siblings of the banyan tree stood unharmed and were flourishing with the mother stem feeding them with its numerous and wide roots speared in depth beneath both the villages. They were not concerned about the division, conflicts or anything else.

With the precaution arrangements in advance, both villagers had somehow successfully over came with the challenge. Some minor casualties of aged and weak children lost their lives in the wrath of sun and otherwise the episode of that calamity of nature went on without much more destruction.

But a new problem has born. The merchants who went to ship in their trading goods were forced to return with their empty carts from Maji village. They denied access to Garu by the fighter guards of Danab through Maji. There was no other way left in alternate.

"Don't ever try to cross through our village. If you come again, these carts will be made your coffins."

They were told. When they returned, they reported to Beera and Gori respectively.

# CHAPTER

**B**eera convened a joint meeting of the leaders of fighter groups of both villages.

"The Maji men are exploiting the worst moments of misery fell on us. Get your skills of fight renewed and prepare for an attack. A befitting reply should be given to those cowards. They are now vomiting bitter out of the last feast of defeat offered by our forefathers in their unsolicited visits with greedy eyes on our soil."

Beera paused for a while and continued:

"Our challenges are multiple; the unrest in our houses due to the cards and wine, the draught which we somehow faced successfully and shortage of commodities and now the inviting conflict of Maji. We need strong and effective striking strategies."

Gori said in thought.

"Yes, when it comes, tragedies ride on convoy. We made it possible to meet the challenge of draught with our collections. The wells bore water to the thirst of our people and pets. If it dries out the wells, we could fetch water from the lake at the far end of our boundary with those carts at our disposal. It was not a task that looked impossible"

Gori asked: "What about the Maji men and the cards?"

"We must start to renew our fighters with training and motivation. For the cards, I have a plan"

"Who amongst you men holds knowledge of cards? Beera continued to ask.

"I know it."

Kanu said. He was a leader of a group comprising the households comprising Litta and his neighbors within Bali. Kanu was Liita's son.

"And among your?"

Beera asked looking at the women group.

"It's me who know it" said Beena who was the daughter of Shila.

"Alright; both of you remain here after dispersion of this conclave."

Beera found a bit of shadow of sadness in Gori's face. But he continued to say:

"Then we are going to disburse now. Prepare for the trainings and if water got dried in the wells send the carts to fetch it to the lakes. It seems that rains will come after our victory over our eternal enemy. Tell the men within your command not to be panic and inspire them to face the threats. Please go through reinforced trainings."

After disbursing the meeting, he called both Beena and Kanu.

"Both of you go and bring me your pack of cards. Get me the newest ones" asked Beera to both of them.

Both went out in haste and brought the cards as Beera asked.

"Thank you. Now you go to your homes and come early in the morning to me. I will say how you will play with these cards."

Both the youngsters went along to their homes.

"What are you going to do with them?" Gori asked.

"My dear, don't be so impatient and intolerant. Just wait and see my game plan"

Gori relieved with his heeling words for the while but she was always doubtful about the sincerity of Beena and Kanu.

Beera was collecting everything in its details through his trusted friends. So he was aware of the undercurrent flowing in paradox with an intention to revolt. He marked all the people involved in the process out from both the villages.

"Gori, there are so many in our villages who should be punished with their misdeeds; but not now. We have to tap their existing potentials we imparted with them. They are in many; spread along under both of our domains. I can read your mind of concerns. Wait for the apt moment."

"What if they pre-empt us?" Gori asked in anxiety.

"No, they will not try because they are aware of the mightiness of our power as we moves in unison. They are waiting for a conflict amongst us or with our enemies."

"And what are you going to do with the cards?"

"Good, do you know the cards?" Beera asked.

"No. I did not put any interest in them."

"Then you should. I will guide you on cards."

Beera taught her about the game. She understood them thoroughly. It was so simple a game with three cards served to each player and bidding blindly to bet a sum of one's choice. When demanded to show cards, the winner grabs the bet with his high graded set of three cards over the opponent's lower grades.

"Look now, you should keep in mind one thing. I am going to mark every card from the pack they are bringing so as they can identify them in blind when it served. They can bid according to their grades blindly supposed to be not read the cards as they are kept their faces flipped down unseen and defeat their opponents."

"Do you mean to apply cheating?" Gori asked in surprise.

"Yes, there is no way left to us to contain this tragic evil. It is better to cheat them rather leave them to spoilt"

"And what should I do with this knowledge?"

"Both of them will be asked to play in their respective villages and challenge everyone who are victorious so far and grabbed others holdings and earnings. Anybody who tasted success in cards will not dare to withdraw from a challenge to play. They will ultimately loss their bets to Beena and Kanu."

"Do you know that they are in love?"

Gori said with a smile.

Beera also smiled.

"Yes, I know it. Let them carry it on. They will marry in hell. When it is found that they are in possession of the bundle of fortune grabbed fully from the gamblers, you just ask them to train you in cards pretending you are ignorant and have a game there after to rob them of their holdings. We will give them back to their real owners who are straying in the streets with broken hearts after obtaining assurance that they will not ever touch the cards in life."

"Brilliant! You are so great and noble in mind."

"You are lovely and brave too, my dearest."

Beera said with smile and he went close to her. He lifted her face in his hands and looking sharply in to her eyes. She too looked in his and the warm air of his exhalations stroke her eyelids... she slowly closed them and moved closer to him and embraced him.

"Gori" he called.

"Beera...what is going within me? I am disturbed... and always wants to be with you...is that love?"

He held her tightly with the hands encircling in her waste and kissed her cheek and lips...

"Yes, I love you Beera. I could not live without you."

"Me too my dear...I love you very much" and he was going wild in his kisses and began to drive his hands throughout back of her body. He pulled her slowly downwards to lie in the floor. She obeyed and Beera disrobed her and with his hands applied mild caresses and his lips offered lovely kisses from her sharp nose projecting beautifully upwards which always lured him a lot since he met her. He kissed her downward to the toes...her solid robust breasts lured him to bite its buds of nipples and he bit those cherry balls alternately...she was giggling and slowly screamed in the pleasure which she never experienced earlier, and she was in her peak of passions when his fingers crept downwards below her marvelous abdomen while his eager lips were browsing downwards to be swirled in to the whirlpool of her deep naval...

"Oh Beera, give me, give me the whole of you! I can't, I can't wait anymore" she moaned in wild desire...Beera was also coming out from within...and he entered into her through her fluid wetness, breaking the thin fortress of her virginity forcing her to moan again in pain and his pace was growing fast and faster... And they become inseparable one-self....in that solitude of darkness within the hut.

Kanu and Beena reported to Beera the next morning.

Beera described them what to do after making invisible marks on each playing cards and showed them how to read without having let their opponents notice the reading in hide.

Grieving lost gamblers swelled in numbers. They gathered in lines to pray for help before the heads of their villages Bali and Likha. Beera and Gori asked them to keep quiet and said they should suffer for their greed and laziness. They disbursed in despair; confessing their guilt.

"Alright, I have won my bet with you two. Now please go, children, to your homes with a mind of peace. You lose nothing but the sweats of others who were foolish to play. You win our hearts and will be rewarded."

Beena and Kanu were disappointed. 'This bitch knew everything and cheated us. We will not spare you' they resolved in their minds and went back.

The losers got their holdings back. All of them were happy to spell out the oath that they will not ever play cards. Thus the unrest grasped those settlements went in hide.

The draught and famine did not affect the settlement in its severity due to the advance precautions. Water was available at the wells. So they concentrated on their practices to renew their talents to resist and fight.

# CHAPTER

eera once again called a conclave.

He began to address thus:

"My dear men, we have come so far winning out all the challenges put up in our settlements by destiny with outstanding determination. It is a great relief that the draught is starting to diminish with the winds brings in some wet clouds over near the sky above us. The major problem of unrest out of gambling is somehow tackled. So far, it is so good.

"Now it is remaining the terrible one at distant. It should be faced with great zeal and bravery. We have to ship out ourselves in carts which are limited with us in numbers. So we have to make a strategy. Our processions will be in two phases. The first one with two groups will reach Maji earlier than the other, and the rest will follow and join them later.

"We would have to shuffle the groups with a re-arrangement."

He called out the names of the people who were marked by him earlier who were supposed to be involved in the dissident activities. They made to one group. Kanu entrusted to lead the group along with Beena. He also deployed five of his trusted aids, who were brilliant in defense, into that group.

Another group was formed with the stalwarts of a few who were specialists in defenses with their shields. They belonged to Likha men who were colleagues of Beera at Garu. They were asked to lead from the front with the three men confined to the cells in punishment and throw them towards the Maji men when they face them.

The rest of the huge force will follow the earlier two groups and will unleash a joint attack on Maji.

'How nice an idea;' Gori exclaimed. The leaders are perfect in defense. Their followers, the traitors who are following will try to defect and attack our own leading men from the back but they will defend themselves with their superior skills. Then we will finish the traitors and forward to Maji. Good plan.' she was happy to think so.

Beera hinted every leaders of the group except the second one about the possible revolt and to be prepared to defend themselves from front and rear. He said that the first front of the procession towards Maji will be a fake one. It is just a dummy front to attract the entire attention of his opponents. They will surely fight to release the captives whom they are looking for the past so as to consulate their grieving relatives.

He further delivered a speech with utmost emotions to raise their motives and confidence. Then he dismissed the conclave after informed them with the day and time to proceed.

The outcome of the conflict was delightful. Every of their plans and schemes of strategy brought success. First they finished the revolting fellows and finally claimed victory over Danab's men. He was spared with his life with stern warning that nothing with ill mind will be created ever.

With thrilling glory they returned homeland.

# CHAPTER

**B**eera went to pray along with Gori to the deity at the priests' seat.

"Don't you seek a priest to assign the seat?" Gori asked.

"No, this will be converted in to a school where our children in the villages will study"

"Then where will you go to offer your prayers?"

"I will offer them within myself in private"

"What will happen to the scriptures?"

"It will be preached to the children. They will study it and follow according to their wisdom."

And then they together went to the Baba's hut. There, Beera found the bundle covered by the cloth left by Baba. He found the scriptures. The shape and look of them differed with those he found at the priests seat. But its contents never confronted. He inhaled a deep breath and said to Gori:

"The omen of love…"

"What?" Gori asked curiously.

"Yes dear, these and those left with us at our priest's seat are the same scriptures. These scriptures uphold the sanctity and necessity of understanding and practice of divine love. It preaches to disburse love. Those supposed to interpret with them were biased and rigid in their selves. That caused the miseries and mistrust. These scriptures will lead us to marvelous world of love when it is opened up let adapted according to the demands of changing time and it will become the tools of oppression when it is kept in the darkness of indoors. So let it be open to the hearts of new generation. There it will flourish or perish as it worth."

The snakes began to sneak in to the lands of Bali. Not a single one of them faced the threat of hurt. There they began to harvest the harvesters according to the laws of nature. The number of rats and mouse began to diminish.

Clouds loomed over that settlement with their ballooned udders longing to milk the cups down the earth. It rained well over the lands. Water filled the lands and spilled, flowed and flooded the fields. Plants and trees bathed in joy. Animals and reptiles sighed in relief. Thirsty hearts burnt within humans wet in cool.

Beera brought out Gori from her house. They went through the street and come out near the foundation of that old banyan tree. He showed his index finger towards there and said in warms voice:

"Look"

Gori glanced slowly. She found the siblings growing in unison. There bottom stems joined together to become one tree. Up above the height of stems, they swung in two branches seemed longing to embrace each other.

She grasped him with her warm hands and said:

"They had united!"

"In love, like us…"

They get in to Beera's home were Janu, Beera's mother, received Gori as the first bride of the newly born Likhabali. Amongst the onlookers, most of them were glad and jubilant but a few had raised their eye brows in distaste.

-0-0-0-

///saraswati namasthubhyam, varade kaamaroopinee, vidyarambham karishyami sidhirbhavathu me sadaa///

-0-0-0-

Printed in the United States
By Bookmasters